PRAISE

BOB AND THE AFTERLAND

Bob and the Afterland

by Michael G. Charles

ISBN 978-1-64663-357-9

Published by

 köehlerbooks™

3705 Shore Drive
Virginia Beach, VA 23455
800-435-4811
www.koehlerbooks.com

BOB AND THE AFTERLAND

MICHAEL G. CHARLES

VIRGINIA BEACH
CAPE CHARLES

To all our friends and family who are in the Afterland.

CHAPTER 1

IT'S A BEAUTIFUL OCTOBER day in Richmond, Virginia, and it's the last one I will ever spend on Earth. I'm driving my old green Toyota Tacoma pickup over the Nickel Bridge crossing the James River. To my right, the river lazily meanders eastward towards downtown. It is strewn with rocks of all sizes scattered across its width and punctuated by a few small islands. The water courses around these but flows gently, as there is very little drop over these few miles. I can see people sunning themselves on the rocks.

In October, the river is low, allowing adventurous souls to wade from rock to rock until they find the perfect oasis on which to lay out a towel and read a book. Years ago, I did some studying there—an anatomy book in one hand and a Rolling Rock beer in the other. I learned the carpal bones of the wrist as well as the subtle hops of a good lager.

As I reach the end of the bridge, the road takes me up a slight rise to the toll booth where I toss in my thirty-five cents—yes, it's no longer a nickel anymore. The leaves have turned shades of orange, brown, and yellow. The sun strobes through the trees like an old silent movie, and the dry smells of autumn surround me. I pass Maymont Park and then, on my left, the Carillion of Byrd Park where the fall art festival is setting up. Another memory hits me.

I'll admit it. My mind wanders when I drive. This makes my wife, Judi, crazy. Everything brings back memories of old haunts. When my family is with me, they are quick to remind me that I have already pointed these places out—many times before.

My mind drifts back to when I was in medical school. A few close friends and I had climbed the fence around Maymont Park. The park covers a hundred acres and surrounds its namesake mansion built in 1890 on a hill overlooking the river. It includes many formal gardens, an arboretum, and some local wildlife habitats. The park was closed after a winter storm when we scaled the locked gate. Leading down from the front door of the mansion was an ideal sledding hill. It was steep enough to give a thrill but not enough to break bones. There was a forty-degree drop that allowed you to build up speed followed by a flat area crossing the road leading up to the mansion. On the far side of the road the hill dropped suddenly and steeply for twenty yards followed by a long more gradual slope to the bottom of a small valley.

On that glorious day, our toboggan broke through the virgin snow compacting a path that became slicker with each subsequent run. We took care to avoid the occasional tree, understanding that 'steering a toboggan' is an oxymoron. Our speed and distance increased as the three of us wrapped our legs and arms around each other, hunching down to improve our aerodynamics. The final reward after multiple trips was a drop into the partly frozen creek bed at the bottom and eventually hot chocolate and peppermint schnapps back at our house.

I shake off the memories and am soon passing the jogging track, following the road around the reservoirs, skirting Boat Lake, and turning onto the Boulevard. Life is good. I have a beautiful wife who is my soulmate. When I say *soulmate*, I pretty much mean she compliments all of my traits and tolerates me incredibly. I also have three perfect kids. I might be biased, but they really are perfect.

We live on a dead-end street in the Westover Hills neighborhood on the south side of the James. The house overlooks Riverside Road, which winds its way along the southern shore of the river. It's a two-story brick house built in the late 1980s and has all the frills you would expect from that era, including a one-car garage with an old workshop, two and a half bathrooms with pastel tiles of pink, light blue, and green, and a finished basement with an old pool table flanked by our furnace and the washer and dryer. In the winter you can see the James River through the barren trees. We might be able to advertise a *riverview* if we ever sell the place, but I think that would be pushing things.

A small path cuts through the trees as it descends to the James River Park. It is well worn by my shoes and the four paws of our maltipoo, Skippy. He loves the water, the smells, and most of all the freedom that comes with our walks. When I look out over the James, I can't help but think of its path—a gentle slide eastward to Hampton Roads, emptying into the Chesapeake Bay, and finally feeding the Atlantic Ocean. Whenever I feel too full of myself, this grand river, the birthplace of our nation, brings things into perspective, dousing me with humility.

Skippy has brought more joy to our house than anything my family could have imagined. Having five humans cohabiting a house is probably one of the most challenging endeavors that the universe could conceive. You mix sexes and generations together, add routine stressors, throw in some occasional random boyfriend breakups, bully experiences, add a dash of, "You should have known what I meant," and the result is an infinite complexity of . . . *aaaghh!* Little Skippy—part maltese, part poodle—is the diffuser. He pretty much takes the nitroglycerine and makes it inert.

So our lives are on cruise control, but in a good way. We are blessed, as many are not born into a world of opportunity. Some emerge with the thinnest of hope, their destinies decided by the color of their skin, the country of their birth, or the decency of their parents. Their purity can be corrupted by the reality of their lives or brought to a premature end by circumstances they have no ability to control. As I look around, I need to thank whomever, daily, for what we have. The *whomever* has always been a challenge.

When we talk of fate and God, emotion seems to override logic. Don't get me wrong, logic can certainly lead towards God. It's hard to explain who we are and how we got here without a higher power being brought in. Nevertheless, as we work to survive our daily struggles, the overall conscription of the universe takes a back seat. I was raised in a churchgoing family, but even then always had a questioning mind.

Thoughts about my belief system lead me back to the here and now. As I said, I am living the dream, one filled with welcomed encumbrances, such as driving to a CVS pharmacy in the Fan section of Richmond to get a prescription filled for my beloved wife's migraine medication. As I go north on the Boulevard I cross its bridge over I-195, the only section of the road without a median. As I do, a delivery truck has a catastrophic failure of the control arm on its front axil. It swerves head-on into my truck with a combined collision speed of 70 mph. Pretty much nothing I can do. Big *bang*, and then everything goes black.

CHAPTER 2

I AM NOW FLOATING. That's the best way to describe it. Thinking of me in a bubble doesn't really do it justice. The first thing I notice is that I can sense other *bubbles* around me— bubbles to the sides, above, and below. I know they are present, but right now I cannot interact or communicate with them, yet I don't feel threatened. Like me, they are in a suspended state.

I know who I am, and I have memories. I can remember everything up to the point the delivery truck swerved in front of me. I even have vivid memories of my entire life—and it scares me. Imagine your whole life in a file cabinet with access to thousands of folders and files harboring all the glorious and gory details. There are some great times of course, but some of the junk I have suppressed for years. It's all rushing back now. I don't have a choice.

Luckily, I think most of my experiences were pretty good. I messed up a bit, but I also did some pretty darn good shit. Being a family doctor, I affected a lot of lives. Most of these interactions were positive, thank heavens. *Heaven? Wait a minute . . . is that where I am?*

I am dead back on Earth. That is a certainty. I am conscious, *alive,* but where? This place is nothing like the Heaven I learned about in church growing up. No Pearly Gates, no clouds, no angels . . . pretty much nothing but bubbles. *Uh oh! Is this freaking Hell! Shit!* No, wait, sorry, I didn't mean to say that. If this is Heaven, I just screwed myself over. I guess if it's Hell, it doesn't really matter anyway.

Getting back to just floating around. I started taking inventory again. The more I assess my situation—*Heaven or Hell?*—the better I feel. I think I did much more good than bad while on Earth. I helped a lot of people as a family doctor. It was nothing like the TV shows, dramatically cracking chests or, like in *House,* making obscure diagnoses to save people at the last minute.

I saw patients with chest pain they thought was heartburn and made sure they got into the cardiologist to get the treatment for the heart blockage they were not aware they had. Not dramatic, but it kept them alive. Sometimes it was just controlling their blood pressure or diabetes to give them extra years on Earth. Other times it was getting proper testing or immunizations that prevented them from dying of cancer or pneumonia. You really don't know how much it actually helps, but I like to think that it helped a lot.

I also think we did a pretty good job with our kids. As I said, they turned out well. Taking all that into account, I figure I'm more likely on my way to a good place instead of everlasting damnation. I also have a strong feeling that where I am is the only place, that there is not another option.

Some kind of portal has just opened. It's hard to explain, but it's like I am in the present somewhere—but I am not. I float over a scene and I know right away what's going on—I'm at my funeral.

CHAPTER 3

ALTMEYER FUNERAL HOME WAS run by Jimmy Altmeyer ever since his dad had passed on the reigns. His family lives in our neighborhood and we had run into them a lot. It was weird having a couple of beers at the local bar with the guy who I knew would eventually be overseeing my funeral. It makes it easier to digest when you consider that he is truly one of the nicest guys you will ever meet. Never forgets a name, which is a must in his business, I guess.

Jimmy doesn't look like the classic funeral director. He's very handsome, but not in a Gomez Addams type of look. He's more of a surfer-dude mortician. *Hey, wouldn't that be great sitcom!* Jimmy should check into that. Anyway, the Altmeyers have a few funeral homes around the Southside of Richmond. They have a small flagship building in the neighborhood and a few bigger ones closer to the city. It looks like I made the cut to use the bigger one. The place is packed! Maybe I wasn't such a bad guy after all. I don't have an ego anymore, (and no id for that matter), but it is nice to see I'm missed.

I can see my family up front, and even though I don't have one anymore, my heart aches. It's a closed casket funeral—I guess I was messed up pretty good in the accident. The casket is flanked by some standard flower arrangements, but also by some of my favorite beers! *Great job family!* There are also tons of pictures— one of our family at the beach in Nags Head, one of some of my closest friends and I celebrating the Packers Superbowl win, one of Judi and I at a Valentine's Day party, and many others.

It is a surreal feeling seeing myself, albeit in a closed casket, being remembered and mourned by those I just left. To me, it was just a few minutes ago when I hit the truck. I get a feeling of finality, though. I'm not coming back.

Chloe, my daughter, is inconsolable. She just turned fifteen, is mid-height with dark, shoulder-length hair, and a quick, easy laugh. She and I were always close. She was my only daughter and a classic Daddy's girl. We had many daddy-daughter dates even up until I died. One of my fondest is a road trip to the old Waterside entertainment complex in Norfolk, and the now defunct Jillian's restaurant. It was a large establishment, basically a Dave and Busters knock-off with a multitude of games, plus a nice bar with good food. You might know the kind of place; you win ten thousand tickets and get to trade them in for a toy bow-and-arrow or a set of shot glasses.

We had finished our arcade games and were sitting outside on the second-floor deck overlooking the Elizabeth River. The ships in the Portsmouth Shipyard dry docks on the other side were under tarps wrapped by scaffolds getting sand blasted and then ordained with new coats of marine paint. There were gray Naval ships in the drydocks, and the massive Carnival Cruise ship *Magic*, which was getting an overhaul. Carnival would occasionally cruise out of Norfolk for Bermuda or the Bahamas.

As we sat at the small table with an umbrella screening the bright August sun, a tugboat, or the Norfolk-Portsmouth ferry shuttling foot passengers between the two city waterfronts, would occasionally pass by. Chloe was just about eight at that time. I had my Guinness, and she sipped her lemonade. Guinness was one of my favorites. When poured correctly it leaves a light nitrogen infused head. As I drank, a foam mustache lingered on my upper lip.

Chloe loved it. "Daddy, look! You have a mustache! What does it taste like? Can I taste it? Please?"

"I don't think you're going to like it honey. Beer is an acquired taste."

"Pleeeaaase!"

"Oh, alright," I relented, as daddies have a tendency to do more often than not.

She came around to kiss me just to check it out, leaving with a sour face after tasting the beer. No 'I told you so' from me. I'm already missing our daddy-daughter dates.

As I gaze upon my funeral, I can see my daughter is struggling. I can get close to her, but that is all. I cannot touch or feel. I think I must be some sort of a spirit, but there was no way I could affect anything or manifest in my old world. I even try to flicker a candle on the altar, but nothing. *So much for all the ghost movies out there!* It's really hard not to be able to give her a Daddy hug to make her feel better, as I had done so many times in the past.

The rest of my family is crying too, and even I choked up a bit. Our friends and family are there, along with a lot of my patients. My practice always had a bit of a small-town feel. Though Richmond is a metropolitan area, my office was in a neighborhood that had a homey style and flavor. My family would always joke that no matter where we were, we ran into my patients. Heck, one time I was in line at the urinals at a Packers-Redskins game at FedEx Field in Washington, DC when I heard someone yell out,

"Hey! Dr. G!" It was Mr. Johnson, one of my long-time patients.

I had written my own eulogy a while ago. Don't laugh, I highly recommend it. One of the hardest things for family members to do is to stand up front of their friends at a funeral and put their loss into words. *So, I did it for them!* I even picked my songs, some tearjerkers, but also "Crazy" by Seal. It reflects some of my philosophy. You have to go a little crazy at times to stay sane.

My eldest son, George, reads the eulogy. He is tall with dark hair, and handsome. He got his height from me, the rest from his mom. He is twenty-two now and out of college. He is able to hold it together pretty well as he reads. The eulogy mentions my wife and kids, of course, but also expresses my appreciation to all the friends I had over the years. After thanking everyone for coming, I finished by apologizing for some of the sappy songs. I don't feel too bad, however. *I mean it's a funeral for God's sake, you should be crying!* The eulogy finishes by telling everyone to enjoy the food and beer.

My portal starts to dissipate when the service ends. Before everything fades completely, I notice an older women coming up to my daughter and telling her that, "You dad is in a better place now." Chloe goes off, shocking the lady by loudly exclaiming, "NO, he is not! The best place for him is right back here with me!"

I think, *You go girl!*

As the portal closes, I'm suddenly startled by a voice right next to me.

"Hey man, what's up? I'm Gabe."

CHAPTER 4

I SUDDENLY PERCEIVE THE presence of another being right next to me but have no clue who or what it is.

"Uh, hey," I fumble. "I'm Mike."

"You're new here, aren't you?"

"I guess so."

"I know what you mean, man. It really screws you up when you first get here. One minute you are doing whatever you are doing and the next thing you know, *bam,* you're here. And then, you start thinking, where the hell am I? Is this Hell? Heaven? Purgatory? Disneyland? I mean, what the fuck! Oops, sorry about the language."

"It's okay, I said the same thing."

"I know, but I really try not to say that word. My mama hated it. Even washed my mouth out with friggin' soap a couple times. I didn't know they could still do that crap. Isn't that corporal punishment? Anyway, this sure proves the existentialists wrong, doesn't it? I mean here we are—wherever we are—if this is even real."

"Yeah, but if it isn't real, what is it?" I ask.

"I've been here a little while, but I still can't figure it out all the way myself. That's the other problem, no concept of time. Could be years or minutes . . . just don't know."

I pause a second. "Are their others here?"

"Of course. It's so big you can't really tell how many, but you know it's a lot. Once you've been here a while, you will start noticing them, they're all over."

I stopped to. I guess the best word to use is, *feel*. Sure enough, I sense other presences around me, but now a bit more distinct. Each has a different aura to it, some really funky though, and I get the feeling they were not human.

"Is God here?" I ask hesitantly.

"Good question," Gabe replies. "We should discuss that sometime. I do know that there seem to be certain hierarchies. At the very center there is a very strong presence. We aren't in close proximity, but you will feel it soon. I call her Big Mamma, not because that is her name. I don't even know if she's a *she* or a *he*. I just get the perception that she's the Big Mamma. There are a lot of entities between us and her, and a lot that are farther away . . . some very, very far."

"So, what brings you here?" asks Gabe, suddenly changing the subject.

"Nothing noble or exciting for me, I'm afraid. I was running an errand and another vehicle crossed over the median and hit me head on. I never had a chance to react. Next thing I know I am here . . . wherever here is. How about you?"

"I'll tell you later," he says. "Let me show you around first."

Right then I think, *What the hell is there to see?* Pun intended. Instead, I just say, "Okay."

Gabe starts floating away and I just float after him. Not sure how I did this. I just go where I want to, which is pretty much to follow Gabe. As we were moving around, I notice something I hadn't before. There are shapes around that aren't the bubble entities, as I have come to think of them. As we move more towards the center—again, hard to know how I know we are going towards a center— I start to see different scenarios. They meld together and don't seem corporal, but more viscous. I recognize some of the vistas, but others seem completely foreign to me.

"Pretty cool, isn't it?" said Gabe.

I'm speechless. As we move on, I see some areas that look like beaches, some that were obviously mountains, some cities, but also some that look like they were right out of the movie *Avatar*. It's crazy. It's hard to explain how they intertwine. The top of a mountain can suddenly transform into an undersea coral reef. Cities and deserts, towns and forests. They all seem to be one.

"*What* is this?"

"We all create this shit," says Gabe. "If we have strong memories of a certain place, we can create it here. It takes practice and you have to be here a while to get the hang of it. The scenarios are constantly changing, but if I want to find a certain area, I can do it somehow. Don't ask me how."

"Did you create any of this?"

"Yeah, I got a few favorite areas I go to. I change it up pretty often but there are a few that I always keep."

"Incredible!"

"Yeah," replied Gabe.

We end up in a neighborhood that looks like it's in a big city. Real hard for me to tell which one, however.

We sit (not sure I can do that) on a curb overlooking a string of row houses.

"Mine is a long story, so you better make yourself comfortable," Gabe begins.

CHAPTER 5

GABE TELLS ME HE was born in Brooklyn and lived on West 8th Street. His parents were Emma and Jimmy Carter—yeah like the president.

"We had a three-story brick row house that backed up to the subway as it passed above ground on its way to Coney Island. You might not know this, but the staging and maintenance yard for the New York Subway is out in Coney. All the cars go out these tracks at some point.

"We had about fifteen to twenty feet of backyard that ended on a fence with barbed wire on it. From there it was a twenty-foot drop to the subway tracks. Even though they were above ground they still had a warning for the third rail . . . that one with all the juice in it. The house was tall but very skinny and attached to the next one over. Small walkways would allow access to the back yards every few houses.

"My mom always had a nice flower garden in the front and grew tomatoes on some wooden trestles in the back. As you entered the front door you would see a staircase straight ahead and a small living room to the right. It was an older house, so it had some small but functional wood fireplaces. One was in the living room and another in the master bedroom. Behind the living room were the dining area and the kitchen. We had a small vinyl table in the kitchen where we usually ate. The dining room was for our big dinners that my mom made sure were mandatory on Sundays and holidays. The house always had the lingering scent of fresh cooked meals. The stairs were narrow except for the first floor, which was more formal. They led up to the bedrooms and down to the unfinished basement, which held our furnace and an old coal bin from the past.

"My parents occupied the whole second floor with their bedroom in the front of the house and a short hallway around the stairs which led to some closets and a study. Their bathroom was the biggest in the house and took up the entire area between the study and the bedroom. My sister's and my bedrooms were on the third floor under the gabled roof. Hers was in the front with a bay window over our entranceway. It was perfect for her as it had a built-in seat she could use to read while giving her a great view of the street out front and our neighborhood.

"As you moved to the rear of the house, a small, shared bathroom was on the right. My room was in the back with a view of the subway . . . well really just a view of the top of the cars as they went by. We had a three-story, wrought-iron fire escape at the back of the house. One of the windows on each floor opened out to it, and I loved to climb out there to watch the trains go by on summer evenings. It was a great place to grow up. My mom decorated it with bargain furniture, but she always added her own touches—handmade pillows, crocheted throws, and all sorts of knickknacks. She had a Jesus statue on one hutch with porcelain Easter eggs that I have no clue where she found. The pictures on the walls were mostly of New York City, but some were obviously from the South. Her parents were from Georgia.

"Mom grew up in Reynolds, a small town south of Atlanta. Her mom was a domestic employee for a middle-class family that owned a funeral parlor. She had an apartment in the back of the house. She cooked, did laundry, and most importantly watched the kids. That's where she met my granddad. He was kind of the deaner for the funeral home.

"What the heck's that?" I ask.

"Well in reality a *deaner* is the technician who helps the medical examiner do autopsies, but the term is also used loosely to describe the person who helps the funeral director embalm bodies. Anyway, that is how my grandma and grandpa met. They lived in Georgia their whole lives.

"When Mom graduated high school, she knew that she needed more than Reynolds. There were not many opportunities for her there, and she had no interest in the ones that were available to her. Never being one to abide by the status quo, she up and moved to Brooklyn. That's where she met my dad.

"He worked as a maintenance man at the Coney Island Amusement Parks. He was the proverbial jack of all trades. He used to take us there at the end of the season after school started. The fall weather was great with warm air still coming off the ocean, but none of the intense heat that plagued the summer. By September, most of the crowds were gone and it was much easier to get us free rides. All the operators knew him, of course, and they were happy to let us sneak on.

"When we were young, we rode all the kiddie rides, but soon advanced to the Wonder Wheel, a unique type of Ferris wheel that has the seats on rails, which allows them to move to the inside and outside of the wheel as it turns. It had great views of the beach and the boardwalk. And of course, there was my favorite—the Cyclone. I still think that's one of the best roller coasters ever built.

"Mom worked at New York Community Hospital on Kings Highway as a ward clerk. She was at Coney Island on the Himalayan ride when my dad first laid eyes on her. He was touching up some paint on the railing and immediately knew my mom was the one. She was with two girlfriends from work and my dad convinced them to meet at the ice cream parlor on the boardwalk after he was done with work. He was a pretty smooth talker back then. They shared some cookies and cream double cones and talked for hours. After that initial encounter, Mom made more and more trips to Coney Island. They were married about a year later and eventually moved from their respective apartments to the house on 8th St.

"My mom took classes in the evening and soon was a licensed LPN. She loved her job running the med-surg ward on the 3rd floor. Being smart and having a strong work ethic, she soon garnered the respect of the doctors and her coworkers. She never forgot how she started, however, and the ward clerks loved her for that.

"I was born two years after they were married. They both worked overtime setting aside every dime they could until they had enough to put a down payment on their new house. It was a dream come true for both of them. Neither had ever owned a house, and neither had ever lived in something so big.

"When I was a baby, I just stayed in their room. With all the stairs, it was always a challenge. My dad built gates for the stairways, the top and bottom of the first floor stairs and the bottom of the stairs to the third floor. Once I was big enough, I got my own room on the third floor. The front room was the best, with the bay window and all, but I wanted the back room. I loved watching the trains go by, and even loved the noise. Some people might think they would keep you awake, but not for me. They were my lullaby.

"One of the first toys I ever coveted was a train set. Toys were a luxury for us, however. Even the HO scale sets were an extravagance. I kept asking over and over, hoping that Santa would bring me one. My mom would say that Santa sometimes wasn't able to give us everything we wanted and that we should remember there were a lot of children not near as blessed as we were who needed things more than we did. Needless to say, my hopes were not high that Christmas, and, though excited, I was not overly optimistic when I came down the stairs to the first floor.

"The tree was in the living room and as soon as I was halfway down, I could see it. I yelled so loud I probably woke up the Jones family next to us. They were older and didn't have kids to worry about on Christmas day anymore. Right in front of me was a shiny HO freight set running around the tree. It was a 2-6-0 steamer with a tender, a flat car, box car, a gondola, and a shiny red caboose. I couldn't believe it!"

"Sounds like a great life," I say.

"It was until—"

Gabe stops talking for a good while. I can't tell if he's sad or just reflecting. It's hard to read people here.

"Things changed when Dad got hurt," he starts again.

"Dad was working on the Mouse at Luna Park. It's a small coaster with cars that seat four people. It is known for whipping you around level turns with short steep drops and camelback bumps. As you go around the turns at the edge of the ride, you feel like you are going to fly off the side. That's part of the thrill, but in reality, the wheels are locked into the small rails. The one hundred-and-eighty-degree turns repeat themselves on different levels till the ride brings you back to the bottom of the hill. Dad was checking a sensor that marked the cars as they came down the second hill. If there was a problem, it would automatically stop the lift hill and engage emergency brakes throughout the ride. As he was leaning over to adjust the sensor gauge, he slipped and fell twenty feet to the ground. My dad was a big guy, but even for him that was a tough fall. He fractured two of his lumbar vertebrae and broke his right wrist.

"Workers comp insurance covered the hospital bills and his rehab. His wrist healed fine, but the compression fractures to his lower spine gave him chronic pain. Once the case was closed by his work insurance, he was pretty much on his own. He had to continue work, even though his back caused pain every day. He never really let us kids know how much he was hurting. Without workers comp, he couldn't go back to therapy or have surgery.

"My dad's father had always worked through injuries, and so Dad was going to do the same. And for a couple of years, he made do. He took Motrin and used his heating pad at night. After a while, the pain became worse. He struggled more and more with his job. His boss was always supportive, knew that my dad was hurting and respected the work he did, even while in pain.

"One day, one of his coworkers gave Dad a Vicodin. It was like a miracle. All of a sudden he could work without pain. He took one a day before work for a week and got a prescription from his family doctor to continue them. That worked well for another year, until he started needing two or three a day to get by. His doctor was not comfortable giving him this much and warned him that these kind of meds were very addictive. He offered pain management, but the copays were too expensive.

"That's when things got bad. Dad found someone a few blocks away from our house that sold him the pills without a prescription. At first it was very doable as the guy didn't charge much for them. My dad paid once every two weeks and got his supply regularly. He hid this from my mom, of course. She knew the dangers of these meds as she saw people admitted to her floor in the hospital on a regular basis, many going through withdrawal.

"After a while, the dealer told Dad the cost was going to double. The dealer said he was having trouble with his supplier and the demand had gone way up. Being the nice guy he was, he was willing to give my dad the pills at the same cost and *loan* him the balance. The *loan* amount built up exponentially, and though my dad tried to pay more each month, he got further and further behind. This went on for months. I can't image the stress it put on him.

"One day we found my dad in the bathtub. He had a bottle of liquor in one hand, which was unusual since he wasn't a big drinker. I am still not sure if he did it on purpose or if he got so down, he didn't know what else to do. The coroner said he had enough hydrocodone in his system to knock out a horse. The blood alcohol level two times the legal limit didn't help."

"Man, that sucks," I interject.

"Yeah, tell me about it," Gabe says. "My dad was a good guy. He worked his ass off to help our family. He wasn't a drug addict. He was just in pain."

Gabe gets quiet and looks forlorn. After a few minutes I gently ask, "What happened next?"

"We had the funeral at our local First Baptists Church on 15th. Mom was always very active with the church. She sang in the choir and even taught Sunday school periodically. Her work schedule precluded her from going every week, but she still was what I would call a regular. The church community rallied around her and helped our family immensely. Even though we slowly got back into our routine, it was hard on my mom. Dad had a life insurance policy at work, but since it had a suicide clause, we never saw a dime. I started a part-time job at the Chinese laundromat down the street. They didn't pay much but were fair to me. My sister was only six at the time. When Mom wasn't working at the hospital, she took some extra jobs doing home health around the neighborhood. We didn't get to see her a lot.

"Even though my sister, Neisha, was very young, she and I were tight. I was responsible for her most nights due to my mom's schedule. I would take her to the beach and Coney in the summer. It always reminded me of Dad. When my mom wasn't working her main job at the hospital, she was doing her home health in the evenings. She would come home around three, make us dinner, then leave by five coming home around ten or eleven. The mortgage still had to be paid.

"Her bosses were understanding at the hospital and tried not to give her evening or night shifts. Nevertheless, circumstances would still occasionally require her to pitch in when others were sick or on vacation. On the days my mom didn't have to work in the evening, I was able to work at the laundromat. I did odd jobs, occasionally packaged the clothes, but mostly delivered to homes in the neighborhood. We got by. It was tough, but my mom was a survivor, the strongest woman I ever met.

"It turns out, Dad owed a whole lot of money to his dealer. That asshole was pissed and started to hassle my mom about paying what was owed. She went to the police, but, of course, there wasn't anything they could do. She told the dealer that she didn't have that kind of money. For a while, he just seemed to drop it. We didn't see him around for many months . . . but he never forgot. In fact, it became a festering wound, growing deeper and deeper until he had to do something.

"One day, I was sitting on my front porch when a car drove up with the brakes squealing. The passenger side window opened, and there were explosions. The next thing I knew, I was here."

CHAPTER 6

I'M SILENT, HAVING TROUBLE fathoming all that Gabe and his family had been through. Finally, a thought hit me.

"Gabe, how old are you . . . or *were* you?"

"Sixteen."

"Damn!" I just floated there.

Finally I say, "I never would have figured. I was sixty-one when I died."

"Yeah, I pretty much had you pegged for an older White guy." Gabe says.

"Wait a minute, I know I probably sound White."

"Duh."

"But I never thought I stuck out that much." I'm bummed and Gabe senses it.

"Hey, man. I wasn't dissing you. I just pretty much knew who you were. White people talk like White people. It's not a bad thing. It just is what it is. Let me guess, you were a bit taller than most, skinny, probably lost most of your hair, and had a small goatee."

"Dag, you nailed it . . . except for the goatee. I tried a beard once and ended up looking like some psycho back-woods dude from *Deliverance*. Never grew any facial hair after that."

"You can tell a lot from how a person talks."

"Are you Black?"

"Yup. You couldn't tell?"

"I wasn't sure but thought you might be. I never really thought of people as colors. In my family practice, I took care of my patients for over thirty years before I died, some spanning three generations. If you would ask me about specific patients, I could tell you their medical conditions, who they were married to, their pets . . . but not whether they were Black, Asian, Hispanic, or White. It was not a focus for me. I remember completing an online study for a talk I attended on unconscious bias. You had to associate a feeling with pictures. They rapidly moved from male to female, black to white. Some were associating the picture to leadership positions, some to education, some to good or bad scenarios. I actually scored with a bias towards Blacks. It didn't surprise me because I really loved my patients."

There was a comfortable pause for a bit.

"Gabe, have you ever seen things back on Earth?"

"Yeah, but not often. It seems like there has to be something that has a lot of emotion tied to it for us to see it. The first thing I saw was my funeral."

"Yup, me too. It was tough, but it had to have been brutal for you."

"Yeah. The whole neighborhood came to my funeral," Gabe says. "There was an incredible amount of anger. It was so stupid. The guy who killed me was caught within twenty-four hours. It was a miracle he wasn't killed by someone from my neighborhood.

"My church is pretty big, and it was filled . . . standing room only. It was really tough for my Mom. Losing a kid is the hardest thing in the world. The question of *why* kept coming back to her.

The parishioners and pastor kept telling her that it was 'God's will,' that I'm in a better place . . . the usual crap. Mom never really recovered though. That kind of hurt never fully heals. I wish I could let her know I'm okay."

CHAPTER 7

TIME IS REALLY SCREWED up here. I mean minutes, hours, years . . . they just have no meaning. Sometimes I just float around with no clue how long. It's weird not having watches clocks, days, nights. I've been wondering about the beginning and end of time.

Aristotle felt the universe was eternal. He said everything is in a state of flux, constantly changing. As a result, he argued that time could never have a beginning or end. That goes against the Bible and most religions, which teach that there was a distinct creation or beginning. Thomas Aquinas also followed those religious teachings. He had enough respect for Aristotle, however, to argue with his peers that Aristotle could also possibly be correct, and that his philosophy was not completely antithetical to the doctrine of the Bible. You can imagine how that went over with the religious leaders.

The Big Bang Theory is backed by cosmic radiation background levels and would seem to also support a defined beginning. The argument among skeptics always comes back to this question: How can something be created out of nothing unless there is a driver or ultimate being who set chaos into motion to create what we have in our universe? When time does not matter, you have a lot of it to ponder these things.

Gabe has been great, and I try to bump into him whenever I can. We discussed tons of stuff like this—even though he is technically just sixteen.

Things can change quickly here. While I am floating around contemplating time and Aristotle, that funky portal thing opens up. It shows my daughter getting married, and I recognize that she's in Virginia Beach. We had vacationed there quite a bit over the years. It looks like my family moved there after my death. I don't blame them; there would have been a lot of painful memories in our old Richmond house. Everyone was at the Star of the Sea Catholic Church located a block from the ocean on Pacific Avenue. It strikes me that, even though I didn't practice organized religion, I had always been admittedly fascinated by it.

I grew up Methodist and Presbyterian and married into the Catholic faith. Throughout my life, I experienced traditional Christian teachings, more radical evangelical versions that required people to be *born again*, and the staunch history-laden traditions of Catholicism. I had taken all this in, but my questioning mindset persisted.

The Star of the Sea takes up two blocks and includes elementary and middle schools with a gym. The main building is a semicircular nave that was built in the more modern style of newer Catholic churches. The pews face the altar like pie slices and the fourteen Stations of the Cross are attached to the walls at the circumference. There are flowers everywhere, and not an empty seat.

Chloe looks beautiful. A full white gown, set off the shoulders with a mid-length train and just a few flowers in her hair. I wonder when she said *yes to the dress*. Judi and Chloe liked to watch that show a lot. I always kept yelling out, *"Say no! Say no! It's too frickin' expensive!"* Anyway, she looks great.

I don't recognize the groom of course. I'm guessing they met in college. He looks decent enough. I would have loved to grill him, however! That's the dad's job. Ask him those questions that will make him uncomfortable. You know, like, "Did you know that unfaithful husbands vanish all the time?" or "I have uncles that can take down a deer at a thousand yards. Just saying."

Judi also looks great. She hasn't really aged much. Still must be working out all the time. My sons, George and Jeff, are also here. *Wait! George is married?* When the heck did that happen? How did I miss that? I can't figure this place out. There should have been a portal! Anyway, Chloe's ceremony is great and I would have cried if I had eyes.

The portal follows them to the reception at the Old Cavalier on the Hill. Looks like my life insurance and pension were pretty good! The Cavalier Hotel was originally built in 1927 in the shape of a *Y* with the stem facing the Atlantic Ocean. It is on a hill with a grand yard stepping down to Atlantic Avenue, and its own private beach club. Originally, it had 135 rooms in its seven stories. Looks like it recently went through a complete renovation with updates to all the rooms and a complete refurbishing of the restaurants and indoor pool.

The reception is in the Raleigh Room, which was on the first floor in the wing facing the ocean. To the left are double doors opening to the indoor pool, and to the right and out the front were verandas overlooking the gardens and the ocean. A gorgeous place. They have a nice little combo playing some standards as the guests fill the tables both inside and out.

I watch for a while and then things just fade out. I feel Gabe's presence.

CHAPTER 8

"HEY BRO, CONGRATS! SHE is beautiful," says Gabe.

"Yeah, thanks. I know. I have—*had*—a great family."

"They're still your family, Mike."

"Right. I know. But how come the portals only open up for some events and not others? Even if they are happy times?"

"I don't know actually. I wondered that myself."

"Gabe, tell me about who or what else is up here. I mean I know Big Mamma is at the center, but what are all these other presences that I can feel around here?"

"Well, we are in the largest section. I call it the Milky Way. This is where most of us end up. The people here lived their lives in a good way. They made mistakes but had their hearts in the right place. There is no true evil here. That lies in the outer reaches beyond the vast space I call no man's land."

Out of the blue he asks, "Have you ever heard of Avicenna?"

"No. I don't think so."

"He was an Arabic philosopher who challenged the traditional Islamic teachings. He believed Aristotle was right when he said the soul is separate from the body. He used the *flying man* analogy to bolster his stance."

"Hey, I've heard of that," I say. "That's the argument that if a person was blindfolded and suspended in the air without being able to feel anything, that person would not know they had a body, but *would* know they had a *self* or *soul*, proving that the soul is distinct from the body."

"Exactly!" Gabe continues. "Our presence here proves that the dualists—those who believe the soul and the body are separate— were right. Rene Descartes took it one step further and stated that the soul was immortal. Anyway, Avicenna was attacked by Orthodox Muslims who believe that the whole person, both body and soul, are resurrected to enjoy the afterlife."

"Surprise, surprise," I say.

"Yeah, not one of the most tolerant religions," Gabe adds. "Anyway, this guy Avicenna was brilliant, even as a child, and became a well-respected physician and philosopher. His death was suspicious, however. Some say that he could have been poisoned."

"Organized religions can really screw things up at times, can't they?" I note. "They can do a lot of good, but I hate the fact that they can be so rigid. They don't embrace questioning minds, even when confronted with logic. There are examples of this throughout history—Copernicus being chastised for his belief that the Earth revolves around the sun, witch hunts, ethnic cleansing, the conversion of the Native American—"

"Not to mention how people pervert religion to promote prejudices and exclusivity," interjects Gabe. "Churches promoted segregation. Radical Islam has killed hundreds of thousands in the spirit of Jihad, or holy war."

"And don't forget the Crusades. Close to three million

barbarians were killed in the name of Christianity," I say.

We just float for a bit, chewing on all that. I break the silence by asking Gabe, "What about getting closer to Big Mamma? I can sense other presences there, some which are really different, though I can't say why."

"The closest to Big Mamma are the innocents—infants and babies who died. Their souls are the purest."

"That begs the question of the innateness of good vs evil," I say. "Their purity would support the argument that we all start out innocent and are then corrupted by our experiences. And the bigger question about free will. Are the *evils* as you call them, destined to become evil, or do they choose that on their own?"

"Predestination sucks!" says Gabe, a little more passionate than I would think necessary.

I realize that I would need to explore that later, but for now I responded, "Totally agree! Even the staunchest religious conservatives had to back off it. They watered it down when they realized how stupid it was. If everything is truly predestined, then there is no free will, and good cannot be distinguished from evil."

"Why do you say that?" asks Gabe.

"To do good or evil requires choice. If we do not have the ability to choose, then who is to say what is truly good or truly evil? To act requires conscious decisions which we make every day. Voltaire is one of my favorites on that point. He believed it was important to doubt every fact and to challenge authority. Governments should be limited and free speech sacrosanct. I have always thought that, but not in a radical White trash sort of way. Do you know how I would fix our US government Gabe?"

"How?"

"Three things. Universal health care coverage—not Medicare for all. The government screws enough stuff up already. We need to have a few national insurance payers who are mandated to cover everyone with some healthy competition. The second is a flat tax.

Right now, the tax system is crap. The very rich find loopholes, the middle class are declared *rich* by the liberals and taxed out the wazoo, and the poor are declared *freeloaders* by the conservatives, encouraging distrust in everyone. A flat tax removes all loopholes, has everyone paying the same percentage of their income, and removes a whole shitload of bureaucracy. The third fix is term limits for all politicians. They spend tons of money to get elected, then spend all their time trying to get re-elected. If everyone had four to six years and done, they would spend more time doing what they are supposed to be there for, which is helping us!"

"I would also limit the number of lawyers that could be in politics," adds Gabe.

"Why so?" I ask.

"I don't know . . . to give others a chance. Ones who don't think like lawyers. I am not too fond of them to be honest."

I knew there was more to the story, but we let it drop and just drift for a while until

Gabe breaks the silence.

"I want to come back to the good and evil thing. If there can be no good without evil, will we ever reach a point of pure good? Could we ever?"

I cogitate for a minute. "I would like to think we could. Maybe Big Mamma is that pure good. Maybe in this world we can evolve past the need for evil."

We both ponder that for a long time.

CHAPTER 9

I FEEL A POWERFUL and somehow larger presence descend from above us. I'm not sure how I know it's *descending*, but I do. I look at Gabe.

"Is that Big Mamma?"

He laughs. "No way man, that's just Bob."

As he got closer, I realized something with a certainty, though I don't know why I'm so certain. Bob's not human. Or even from Earth. He's a completely different life form.

I looked at Gabe and stammer. "Where's he from?"

"I know, it really freaks you out at first. You could tell, couldn't you?"

"Yeah, I don't know how . . . but yeah."

"His real name is unpronounceable in our language," Gabe says. "I just call him Bob."

"Where *is* he from?" I press.

"Another world, another solar system, another universe, maybe. I'm not sure. You just know he is not human. He doesn't talk or communicate like us. I'm not even sure how we are communicating to be honest. It's much easier to converse with other humans, but even then, we aren't really talking."

Just then, out of nowhere, Bob is in my head. I guess the closest way of explaining this would be to say we telecommunicated, but even that is inadequate. I will translate what comes to me from Bob as best I can.

"Yo, dude"

Okay, maybe that's not it.

"How's it hangin'?"

Maybe not that either. The impression I get is that this Bob creature is laid back. Like a Rastafarian. Anyway, I like him immediately.

I respond. "I'm doing okay. Kinda getting used to this place. It's pretty different."

"Very much," Bob responds. "These shells are confining. I guess they couldn't really let us completely free, though, could they?"

"I guess not," I stammer. I want him to like me for some reason. He seems like a real cool dude.

Just then, a smaller bubble pops out from behind Bob and barks at me

Snoopy?

I knew him right away. He was my boyhood dog for seventeen years growing up. A mixed cocker spaniel was what they said at the pound, but he was just a little black ball of fur when we got him. Over time he grew up to be about twenty pounds and looked like he had more terrier blood in him.

He bumped right against me, and suddenly a rush of memories emerged.

Snoopy chasing our hamster around in his plastic ball. Snoopy climbing a metal rung ladder to the second story of the addition being built on our house. I remember how he was able to get up the ladder, but of course we had to carry him down. Snoopy walking with me around the block as I built up the courage to ask Ann Schreiber to the prom. Snoopy playing with us in huge piles of leaves. Snoopy barking at the waves to the side of our small speedboat, then suddenly disappearing and popping up swimming in the wake. Finally, Snoopy sitting silently beside me, old and blind, the night before he was put to sleep.

Now here he is! I know it's not logical, but I swear he jumps up and licks me. Also not logical, I gave him a big hug.

"Gabe! You didn't tell me our dogs are here!"

"Yup. They are up at Bob's level. Higher than us. A few horses, dolphins, chimps, and others also. Mostly dogs though. I think there's one cat."

"I love these little dudes," says Bob.

I hold Snoopy close and ask Bob and Gabe, "Who else is up here?"

"Bob knows much more that I," says Gabe.

"What do you want to know?" Bob offers.

"What the hell is this place?"

"I don't know what *hell* is, but this is where we are."

"Okay, Bob. That doesn't really help me much." I start talking to him like he's an old friend. It seems natural.

"We used to be where we were, and now we are here."

"Okay. Now you are sounding like a cross between the Dalai Lama and Zoltar."

"Who is Zoltar?" Bob asks.

"He is a coin operated fortune teller who was made famous in my favorite movie, *Big*," I explain like Bob would know what I was talking about. "Wait a minute! You know about the Dalai Lama?"

"Of course, I have met many of the Dalai Lamas. We have hung out," Bob replies.

I looked over at Gabe. *What the fuck?*

Gabe looked back at me and shrugged.

"Bob, tell me about Big Mamma and where you hang out with

the Dali."

Bob kinda sits back a bit. I notice a few other dog entities were hovering around him.

"The Big Mamma, as Gabe calls it, is the central entity to our *now*. If you think of where we are as a sphere with no boundaries, the Big Mamma is at the center. Next to her are the innocents. After that are those who sacrificed. My people are next with the little furry ones. You are outside us in the biggest region. There's a shitload of you."

Bob doesn't actually say *shitload*. It's my translation.

"Next there is a vast void," he continues. "Very, very far away are the others."

"Who are the others?" I ask.

"They are evil," says Gabe. "You can sometimes feel them, even though they are very far away."

"Do you have evil in your world, Bob?" I ask.

"Good and evil are now and before and forever."

Shit, now he's sounding like Phil Jackson!

CHAPTER 10

BOB AND SNOOPY DISAPPEAR, which just happens in this world. People are there and then they aren't. Screwy. I have so many questions. I get the feeling this is not a bad place, though. I decide that I am going to call this the *Afterland*. I always liked amusement parks and something as crazy as this seems to be an ultimate theme park.

Gabe suddenly pops up, and I ask him why he didn't like lawyers—when alive, that is.

"Oh man, it's not that I don't like all lawyers. It comes back to the trial of my killer."

He takes me to a park-like area—a smaller version of New York's Central Park. We walk by a frozen lake surrounded by banks of fresh snow; ice skaters slowly circle counterclockwise across the blue surface. After that we pass some people above the trail reading on the rocks and others in a meadow playing Frisbee in the sun. No consistency to the weather at all here. Winter and summer mesh together. As we float on, Gabe continues.

"The guy that was my dad's dealer was well known in the neighborhood. He hung out by Adam's Deli on the Avenue. He wasn't a gang banger, but he had a bunch of dudes that attached to him like leeches. All assholes. They had money and liked to flaunt it, but none of them were big time, and the bitches could never leave the hood. For some reason the cops never bothered them.

"The main dope slanger was named Daemon. That's what everyone called him anyway. The car that was used in the drive by that killed me was owned by one of his guys. My sister saw it all from her bedroom. She was reading in her bay window."

"Man, that sucks."

"Yeah, tell me about it. There were a bunch of other witnesses on the street also. The case looked to be pretty much open and shut.

"I watched the trial back then. It opened in a portal. Tons of emotion in the courtroom of course. The whole neighborhood was there. It was at the Kings County District Court in Brooklyn. Talk about an imposing building. This mother was about eight stories high. Looked like a castle. There were big stone arches at the front with wrought iron gates topped by spear heads. I thought that if you are going to trial in this place, it must be for some serious shit. Anyway, the trial didn't really get a lot of publicity. It was just another young Black kid killed by gunfire. Everyone who didn't know us figured it was gang related.

"At the opening statements, the city prosecutor did a good job. She was young and overworked but really believed in us and painted a picture of a good family affected by drugs and then terrorized by an animal. The defense lawyer was well paid and experienced. He, of course, was 'so sorry about the tragedy' and 'really hoped they would find the killer.' He brought up in his opening statement that 'it was a rough neighborhood' and 'maybe I got associated with the wrong people.' He also mentioned how Daemon had a solid alibi and the prosecution did not really have any case against him. I immediately disliked that bastard.

"After the opening arguments something funny started happening. The prosecutor's witnesses—one after the other—suddenly forgot what the car looked like and said they didn't get a good look at the people in it. Obviously bullshit. A few other witnesses were excluded by the judge when the defense lawyer argued prejudice. They were hoping my sister wouldn't have to testify, but it came down to her in the end.

"The prosecutor walked her through what she saw. She was in the bay window seat of her third-floor bedroom reading as she often did. As you remember, this looks out the front of our house onto the street. She said she looked up because a car was driving fast down the street and then hit the brakes hard. She remembered it was a big white car with a hard top and four doors. She saw a man lean out the front passenger window and fire a handgun. At first, she didn't know what was going on, then she saw me on the front steps and screamed. She and Mamma ran out to the front, but it was too late. I had been shot four times."

"Sucks that she saw the whole thing," I say. "I can't imagine how she could ever handle something like that."

"Niesha and my mom are the strongest two people in the world," Gabe says. "I'll never forget when Nee was cross-examined. That day the portal was as sharp as can be. The courtroom was packed, and emotions were high. She was eight years old, but because her testimony was so important, the judge allowed the defense attorney to question her. He was the reason I am not fond of lawyers. His name was Mr. Armani . . . no lie. His clothes cost more than my mom made in six months. A full year if you include his freakin' shoes. Well anyway, he stood up to question Nee, but had no clue what he was in for."

Suddenly, as Gabe recounted the courtroom testimony, it was as if I was witnessing it live.

Mr. A: "Sweetie, I know this must be incredibly hard for you."

Nee: "I am not your Sweetie! Your Honor, please ask the defense to address me with respect!"

Judge: "Mr. Armani, please proceed without any endearments."

Mr. A: "Ms. Carter, I understand this is hard for you, but I want to ask you what happened on that day in April."

Nee: "That bastard over there shot my brother Gabe!"

Mr. A: "Your honor!"

Judge: "Ms. Carter, please watch your language."

Nee: "Sorry Judge, but he did shoot my brother, and he is a bastard. My mamma always told me to tell the truth."

Judge: "Counsel, please continue."

Mr. A: "Ms. Carter, what were you doing that day before your brother was shot?"

Nee: "I was in my room reading in the bay window."

Mr. A: "What floor is your room on?"

Nee: "The third floor, facing the street."

Mr. A: "What book were you reading?"

Nee: "The Autobiography of Malcom X"

Mr. A: "That's pretty heavy reading for an eight-year-old."

Nee glares at him until he looks away.

Mr. A: "I figure you were pretty engrossed in the book. Is that correct?"

Nee: "It's a good book."

Mr. A: "So it might take a minute or so for you to react to something that happened?"

Nee looks over Mr. A's shoulder in shock and shouts, "Oh my God, Look!"

Mr. A immediately swiveled to look behind him.

Nee: "It didn't take YOU a minute to react, did it?"

Members of the jury chuckle.

Judge: "Order please. Counsel may continue."

Mr. A: "So Ms. Carter, you turned when you heard the gunshots?"

Nee: "No, I turned to look when I heard a car speeding down our street and suddenly braking."

Mr. A: "Was that so unusual?"

Nee once again glares at him.

Nee: "Our neighborhood is not a crime-ridden slum populated by gang bangers. Our neighbors all work hard, pay taxes, go to church, and obey the laws. So yes, a car speeding down the street is unusual, and gunshots are NOT something I usually hear."

Nee's voice gets louder. "AND, I would like to say that my brother was not in a gang, did NOT hang out with hoods, and DID NOTHING TO DESERVE WHAT HAPPENED TO HIM!"

Mr. A: "Objection! Your honor, the witness is badgering me!"

The judge looks at Mr. A. incredulously. The lawyer realizes what he said and slinks over to his table to drink a sip of water. After a minute, he returned to the witness chair. I could have sworn he was sweating in his $5,000 suit.

Mr. A: "Ms. Carter, you do agree that you were on the third floor of your house?"

Nee: "Yes, I think I already said that."

Mr. A: "So you really couldn't see inside the car that was close to thirty feet below you, could you?"

Nee: "I saw the hand come out of the passenger's seat with a gun in it firing at my brother."

Mr. A: "But you agree, you couldn't see that persons face or body? Is that correct?"

Nee: "No, but I have seen that hand before. It was wearing a fake Giants Super Bowl ring and the fifth finger was broken in the past."

Mr. A: "And how do you know this, Ms. Carter?"

Nee: "The defendant had been at our house when my father was alive, pushing his drugs on him and taking all his money."

Mr. A: "Objection!"

Judge: "Sustained."

Nee: "You asked."

Mr. A: "So, Ms. Carter, You expect us to believe that you could recognize this hand and ring from the third floor of your house when you only saw if for five to ten seconds, being generous that if was visible for that long?"

Nee: "Yes. One of the advantages of being eight is having eight-year-old eyes . . . 20/10 is the new 20/20."

More chuckles from the jury.

Judge: "Order!"

Mr. A decides to cut his losses.

Mr. A: "I think the jury will have to decide that for themselves, Ms. Carter. No further questions, Your Honor. The defense rests."

The closing arguments are straight forward. Nee is essentially the only witness for the prosecution that would come forward. Though she was strong, it wasn't enough. The jury is out for six hours and acquits Daemon.

CHAPTER 11

OVER THE NEXT FEW years in Earth time, I am able to see several openings in the portal. Some of the best are of my family.

My daughter got married, as I mentioned before, but is now pregnant. My older son had a baby boy, and then my younger son got married also. I'm very proud of all their accomplishments. My daughter moved to New York City, following in my footsteps, going to medical school and then building a thriving pediatric practice. She got interested in medical research and started teaching at one of the best medical schools on the East Coast, New York Presbyterian Columbia University Medical Center, which is north and a bit east of Central Park.

She and her husband live close by on W 176th street right next to J Hood Wright Park. They rent the top apartment of a six-story brownstone and love the neighborhood. The park has a great dog run that their little maltipoo Skippy uses almost daily. He was a legacy dog named in honor of the Skippy we had in Richmond. This Skippy owns the place, even though he is only ten pounds soaking wet. They call him the protector dog. He stands up to any dog at the park, no matter what the size. You can almost translate his barking, *don't come near my masters, bitch, or I'll bite your lower ankle off!*

I still use Earth time as a reference point, because I have no way of gauging its passage in the Afterland. There are no days or nights. The only way we know of the passage of time is by the portal updates.

Anyway, one *time* Bob popped up right next to me. I can never get used to this. Simultaneously, I was transported to a place beyond my imagination. I surmised that we were in Bob's world at one of his favorite places. We were about halfway up impossibly tall plant life. I would like to say *trees*, but they looked more like huge vegetables.

We were at the edge of a large plain covered with an interlocking grid of yellow plant life. It seemed to move on its own, but of course I couldn't feel any wind—or much else for that matter. I did perceive the scent of lilac, but different with a sweeter tinge. Above the plain were large flat beings, or maybe I should say animals, that floated in groups. They looked like large planaria. (I can't describe a planaria – you just need to look it up on your cell phone!) The sides of their bodies undulated as they passed by us.

Bob doesn't do small talk. He immediately says, "Tell me about religion."

I was taken back for a second.

"What do you mean? You don't have religion in your world?"

"No," says Bob. "Gabe tried to explain it to me, but I really have a hard time grasping the concept."

I hesitate, thinking, *Wow, this is a really big issue to try to give in an elevator speech.* So I think back to my comparative religion course in college and begin.

"Religion is based on the premise that there is a higher power—or *God*— that sets standards for beliefs and behaviors that we need to follow. People in my Earth world would worship this deity, and in the past would sacrifice animals or other humans to try to stay in good favor."

"Sounds weird," Bob blurts.

"Yeah, I guess it does, doesn't it? I am probably not doing a good job of explaining."

"Start back when religion first began," Bob suggests.

"Good idea."

I noticed that Snoopy is back hovering around both of us.

"I think religion started as a way for people to explain what they could not understand. Bad things would happen, as would good things. Natural disasters occurred, and pretty dramatic celestial phenomena such as eclipses and comets came totally unexpectedly. People did not have the knowledge base to understand what was happening. They decided that there was someone—or something— that controlled all of this. It could even be a group of *gods*.

"In certain cases, leaders would come forward and declare that animals or people needed to be killed to keep these higher powers happy . . . otherwise bad things would happen. If bad things happened anyway, then they figured they needed to sacrifice more to appease these gods."

"That's stupid," says Bob.

"Yes, but that was all in the past. People on Earth and their religions have evolved over time."

On that point, Gabe pops up.

"Hey guys, you can't talk about religion without me!"

"Bob just asked me to explain it to him. He says you tried, but he still can't really comprehend it."

"That's because it's unfathomable!" says Gabe.

"It's not all bad," I say. "Religion has done a lot of good over the years. Many Earth people have been helped by those who practice modern religions."

"I will admit that our local church has been a great support for my mom and sister. Still, you cannot ignore the harm that organized religion has caused," insists Gabe. "Even now, radical religious zealots in our old world are torturing and killing innocent people in the name of their religion. Some of the religious leaders are even using their station to abuse children."

"Who are these 'religious leaders'?" asks Bob.

"People who are designated by God to translate to the masses what is right and wrong, and how they should live," I explain.

"Why doesn't God do that itself?" asks Bob.

"Then the pastors, priests, rabbis, imams, shamans etc. etc. would all be out of jobs!" interjects Gabe.

"That's a good question, Bob," I say, ignoring Gabe. "The thoughts are that God is so complex that we need help interpreting what he wants us to do. These special designees are *ordained* or picked out, especially by God, to translate things. Some of these people are very highly revered, almost as much as God itself."

"You gotta tell him that there are lots of different religions that believe in different gods who tell people to do different things," says Gabe.

"Why is this?" asks Bob. "Is not the truth, the truth? Is not good, good? Why does there need to be more than one religion or god?"

"Touché," says Gabe.

"That is one of the problems with religion, Bob. Each religion thinks that their beliefs and their God are the only true ones. Battles have been fought over centuries on Earth about that very thing. Many people have been *converted* to the religion of the people who have more power."

"But wouldn't a true God be obvious to everyone? Why would you have to convert people? Shouldn't they already know that this one God is the only one?" Bob presses.

At this time, I would usually say, "Go ask your mother." A few problems with that. Bob might not have a mother. Even if he does, his mother probably couldn't answer the question. And the question is a good one!

"Yes, Bob. That's a very good question. One that philosophy has been trying to answer for eons."

"What is philosophy?" he asks me.

Damn! Of course Bob would ask this.

I take a big breath, at least I imagine I have. "It's a way of trying to explain why we do what we do, think what we think, and believe what we believe," I say, figuring my feeble definition would not make Wikipedia. "That may be for a different discussion, Bob."

"Okay," says Bob. "But this religion still confuses me. It sounds like it is not very logical and can even be harmful. How could it possibly be helpful as you mentioned earlier?"

"Religion is based on *good* and *evil*. Universal truths. The problem is that each religion defines what is good and evil in its own manor without understanding that for good and evil to truly exist and be logical, they must be universal constants and not open to separate interpretations. Saying that, religions still try to strive to do *good* in their own way. Good people, truly *good* people in the universal constant way, have used religion to help others and even have sacrificed themselves to help others. There are stories of this in most religions."

"So shouldn't people strive for this universal good and work together to that end?" Bob asks.

"Out of the mouth of babes," says Gabe.

But I know this was not out of the mouth of a babe. Bob has an intelligence and cadre of experience way beyond mine.

CHAPTER 12

THINGS ARE TRUCKIN' ALONG in Afterland. I meet other beings and run into some friends and relatives now and then. I see through my portals that Chloe delivered a healthy little boy, Billie, and then became pregnant again with a daughter.

Suddenly, while I am thinking about her, a portal opens. And there is Chloe. She was delivering her baby girl, Anne, with a seemingly normal delivery. But I can tell that something is wrong. Chloe is at Columbia hospital in the pediatric ward with her daughter, surrounded by two doctors in long white coats with two residents hovering in the background. Chloe looks worried. Anne is in the bed looking fine, but adults are discussing lab tests. The baby's lymphocyte count is sky high. I can read my daughter's mind, and it is the first place my mind goes—*ALL*—acute lymphocytic leukemia. This is certainly not a death sentence. Kids have a 90 percent survival rate. But the diagnosis does mean chemo and lots and lots of doctor visits. My heart goes out to Chloe and Anne.

When I was alive and found myself presented with challenges or bad news, I always took some solace in music. Afterland, being what it was, immediately transports me back to a small jazz club in the basement of an old school building on West Main Street in Richmond. Jazz seems to always be best in basements and small rooms. My friends and I used to watch a fusion band there called Secrets and, sure enough, I was at our usual table about ten feet from that very band. The room is the size of a classroom with a small bar at one end. It isn't used as a restaurant, only for live music. Right away I recognize the songs and the members of the quartet, even though their facial details seemed blurry.

Bob and Gabe suddenly pop up next to me. I'll never get used to that, still spooks the hell out of me. I'm glad to have them with me, however.

We all just float, or sit, or whatever it is we do, and listened for a while. There is nothing comparable to live music.

Three draft beers appear before us—Sam Adams Boston Lager. Not sure how they got there, but it was appropriate for the venue. I notice that Bob's was emptying fairly rapidly.

"Bob, do you like beer?" I ask.

"It's good," he says.

"Well go slow, we might have a long night here."

I turn to Gabe, "What kind of music do you like?"

"All kinds," he perks up. "Love jazz and blues but also hip-hop and even old school Motown."

"Can't beat that," I agree. "I was in San Francisco for a meeting once and found a place called Biscuits and Blues on Mason Street. The food was good, and the live blues were even better. Turns out the Jack in the Box on the floor above started leaking sewage on them and they had to shut down. The good news is they are back in business. There are only a few blues bars in San Fran now, so I was glad to hear they survived the onslaught. You can't make this shit up."

"Did you play an instrument?" asks Gabe.

"Yup, played the trombone. Started in third grade when I couldn't even reach sixth position. I had to put the slide on the floor and lean back! I got pretty good, usually playing lead or first chair. I was always jealous of the professional musicians, however. I had good technic, tone, and embouchure, but could never get to that upper echelon of the great players. They have a higher level of musical intuition that I couldn't reach."

I notice Bob is on his fourth beer. "Whoa, big fella. Slow down a bit. The night is young."

"I like beer," Bob declares.

I ask Gabe, "Have you ever heard of Stanley Jordan?"

"Yeah, he's a jazz guitarist. A brother if I remember right."

"You got it. Born in Chicago. Brilliant dude. Studied music at Princeton. At seventeen, he won an award at the Reno Jazz Festival. I saw him play once in Virginia Beach at a small club upstairs over Mary's breakfast place on 17th street. He was twenty-two at the time. He uses a touch technique—tapping the strings at the appropriate fret. He didn't invent it, but he took it to a new level, playing more of a legato style than the usual staccato that you hear when guitarist use this. He plays the melody and chords simultaneously on the same guitar. It's crazy. Back when I saw him, he played the old Zeppelin classic 'Stairway to Heaven.' No backup band or combo. He killed it. What really blew me away was when he reached his right arm over an electric guitar mounted on a stand in front of him and—while still playing background on the guitar around his neck—played Jimmy Page's solo with one hand on the electric. *Crazy!*"

Right after Secrets finished up their next song, Stanley appeared in their place! He started right up on 'Stairway' and I watched as Gabe and Bob got blown away just as I had years ago.

We bounced around a few different jazz bars watching some of our favorites – Ramsey Lewis, Keith Jarrett, Ella, Louis. At one point we ended up at a club in Detroit covering all the great Motown classics."

After a few more beers, we call it a night. *Damn it, no nights!* Bob really threw down the beers. I realized that at some point I need to take him to some microbreweries and get him the full experience. When we finally make it out of the last joint at closing, all three of us are floating a bit unsteadily down some street singing a pretty good rendition of "Midnight Train to Georgia."

CHAPTER 13

THE NEXT TIME THAT I encounter Bob and Gabe I have some questions.

"Bob, remember when we discussed *the innocents*? You and Gabe told me that's the group closest to Big Mamma."

"Right," says Gabe. "Those are the beings that died when they just came alive."

"I think he means babies," I tell Bob.

"So, are we truly born innocent?" I ask.

"Why would a new life not be innocent?" asks Bob.

"This is a good example of what we call philosophy, Bob," I say. "Remember, we discussed *philosophy* before, but we kinda dropped the discussion because I had a hard time explaining it. Anyway, the point is, if we are born innocent, why do we become evil? There are some people in our world who say that when we are born, we are predestined to be either good or bad. We cannot control what we become."

"Why would any being be created evil?" asks Bob.

"That's a good question," I say. "We know evil is around us. Does it develop from our experiences or is it internal? If it can be internal, then when does it start?"

"Oh, I see what you're getting it," says Bob. "It is all of those things. Innocence can be lost by the evil of others or it can be destroyed by evil that develops within ourselves."

"I'm good with that. I never bought into the predestination crap," Gabe interjects.

"I'm with you," I say. "But one thing concerns me, Bob. Why are there so many *innocents*? There seems to be a lot more than I would expect."

"I guess it depends when life begins," says Gabe.

"Makes you wonder, doesn't it," I say. Gabe and I shared a look.

"What are you talking about?" asks Bob. "Life begins when we are created."

"It's not that simple in our Earth world, Bob," Gabe says. "We have people arguing all the time about this. Our species relies on a male and a female getting together to create a new being."

"How do they do that?" asks Bob.

"Go for it, Gabe," I chuckle.

For the first time, Gabe is at a loss for words. He stammers a bit. "Well, um, the man lays down with the woman and they make love."

"What is make love?" asks Bob.

I giggle. I know, immature, but I can't help it.

"Um, it's when a man and a woman—" Gabe just trails off.

"Let me see if I can help," I say, coming to Gabe's rescue. "Bob, we have two different sexes that each contribute gametes and DNA to a new being. The male inserts his penis into the female's vagina. His sperm—the transmission vehicle of the DNA—combines with the female's egg which holds the other half of the DNA. This DNA divides and replicates in the female's uterus until the new entity is ready to leave the female and breathe on its own. Bob, how do you create new entities?"

"At a certain time in our lives, some of us develop a new entity within," says Bob.

"Wow, you mean you reproduce asexually? Just by yourself?" I ask.

"Yes, our new being forms inside us until it is ready to survive on its own. Do you mean that only half of your Earth types of beings grow new entities?"

"Well, I never thought of it like that, but yes, only the females of our kind develop new entities."

"That is sad," says Bob.

Gabe and I look at each other. We never really thought of it that way. As males, we understand the burden and dangers of pregnancy but really don't think much of the joy that comes with carrying a child to birth.

"How often do you have problems with your new entities before they are ready to survive on their own?" I ask Bob.

He pauses for a few seconds. "It can happen, but it is very rare."

I sensed he almost whispers this, but of course how can I really tell. I did feel there's something he isn't telling us.

"Do you ever stop the process so that the new entity doesn't stay in your body?" Gabe asks Bob.

For the first time, I see Bob react. He glows a bit and seems to shiver.

"Why would we ever do that?" he asks slowly. "It is an honor to be allowed to create a new being in our world. We would never stop that process once we have been blessed with its creation."

"We actually will stop the process if the female desires not to continue," I say. "I think that could be why we have so many innocents up here."

Once again Bob glows. "But why? Why would someone ever want to stop a new life from being created?"

"It's complex," says Gabe. "Sometimes the female doesn't feel she can care for the new being. Sometimes the new being puts the female at risk of not surviving herself. Sometimes the female is forced to have the new being by an evil male of the species."

Bob just hovers, saying nothing.

"Bob," I ask. "Does having a new being in you ever cause injury or risk to the being who is supporting that new being?"

"It can occasionally happen," he says.

Again, I sense a hesitation in his tone.

"How do you decide who to help or who should survive?" I ask.

"Once the new creation process starts, we consider that we are two entities of equal importance. We try everything we can to keep both alive. Sometimes the older or the newer entity will not survive. Sometimes neither do. It is our goal to keep both alive."

I looked at Gabe. "Makes you wonder."

"Yeah," he says. "I always thought it was the woman's right to choose. What if we are wrong about this?"

"I have always thought that we need to really decide when life does begin," I respond. "We need to remove religion and politics from this and try to answer the ultimate question that matters most. When is a new entity or life actually created? If we can answer that, everything else is not really in question. You can't use the logic that it's not a life until it can survive on its own outside the womb. Current neonatal care has moved this down to twenty-one weeks, but who is to say that newer technology will not allow us to keep a baby alive even earlier. If this is a moving target it should not determine when life begins. We need to find another marker. Is it at conception? That is the real point of no return. If we do decide that is the time, it opens a whole can of worms for in vitro fertilization and the storage of fertilized eggs."

"No easy answer to this, is there?" asks Gabe.

"No, but it is critical that we figure this out, especially if we are wrong. Looking at all these innocents, I am afraid we are."

Bob just floats silently. I am sure he has an opinion on this. I think he felt this was something we needed to fix ourselves.

CHAPTER 14

I FIND BOB AND Snoopy hanging out by a beach. The water here is quite a bit different, though hard to qualify why it is so. The beach itself has something like sand, but it's blue and seems to be a part of the water. I also see the same weird vegetable trees that I saw before with Bob. They seem attached to each other about ten feet off the ground and then expand upward in another layer like a reverse chandelier. It's beautiful.

We're sitting here watching the waves. After a while, I ask a question. Bob is never one to initiate small talk.

"Bob, if you don't mind me asking, how did your life end?"

"Why would I mind?" he asks innocently.

"I wasn't sure—"

"No worried," he says, imitating but not exactly getting my favorite 'no worries' expression correct.

"I died when my new entity left my body and was able to live on its own."

Wow, I think, understanding a bit more of what makes up Bob. "What happened?"

To my surprise, Bob actually explains things. This is probably the most I ever heard him talk at once. Snoopy nuzzles in between both of us while he talks.

"I was overjoyed when I found out I had a new entity in me. Not every one of us gets to experience this. I did everything right and increased my nutrition just as I should. As my new entity grew, I noticed something did not seem to be right. There are some among us who can help us when we feel ill or get hurt. I went right away to seek their counsel. When I was examined, I was told that my new entity had a rare condition that was preventing it from growing. There were ways to help it, but it involved absorbing some of my being to give it sustenance. They told me that it could be dangerous for me, but I never hesitated. My little one had to live. As time went on, I got weaker and weaker. Even though I knew I was fading, I could tell my little one was thriving. I was never happier. Finally, the time came for my new one to leave me and be on its own. I was able to see it circling me in joy, and that was the last thing I remember."

"Man, I'm sorry Bob," I murmur.

"Why?" He seems truly puzzled.

"You didn't get to see your little one grow up at all."

"But I gave it life," he says. "What more could I have wished for?"

We both tune back to the sea. Nothing more needs to be said.

CHAPTER 15

ANOTHER TIME WHILE WE are all just floating around together, I ask Bob and Gabe about the next level out from the innocents. I remember them saying there are not that many entities in this level. Bob explains that these were the ones that sacrificed themselves for others.

"They didn't need to die doing so," Gabe says. "I recognized a lot of the ones from our world who are in that level. I've seen Jesus, Mohammed, Mother Teresa, Abraham, but also others such as Nelson Mandela, Chief Joseph of the Nez Perce, Rosa Parks, Ghandi, Florence Nightingale, Martin Luther King, and Dalai Lama. You also will see a lot of people whom you might consider *normal*. They sacrificed in multiple ways. I saw Desmond Doss once."

"Hey, he's the guy from the movie *Hacksaw Ridge*, isn't he? I loved that movie."

"You got it. One of my favorites also."

"And there are others like him that you probably never heard of like John Robert Fox, Maximilian Kolbe, Salvo d'Acquisto, Richard Rescorla, Arland Williams, thirteen-year-old Jordan Rice—" He trails off. I notice Bob has left. Gabe sensed something was happening.

A portal opens and we're looking at the first floor of Gabe's house. Someone is climbing out of the window and closing it behind him.

Gabe yells, "That's Daemon! What are you doing, you bastard!"

I notice that the doors to the kitchen are closed. I see a small candle lit on the floor.

"What the hell?" I say.

Gabe sees it first. "The stove is on. We have natural gas! That fucker! He's trying to blow them up."

I notice the flame on the floor and it all fits. Commercial natural gas is a combination of methane, ethane, and heavier gases such as propane and butane. The propane and butane are usually removed and sold separately in a liquid form. New York natural gas is 98 percent methane, which is the lightest of the gases—lighter than air. The gas from the stove will rise to the top of the room slowly and then displace the air until it reaches the flame on the floor, which will ignite it.

"Oh my God!" exclaims Gabe, "we've got to do something!"

"What can we do? I wasn't able to even flicker a flame at my funeral!"

Just then we hear a dog bark.

"That's Rusty!" says Gabe.

We watch as the portal moves upstairs. Rusty has come down from the third floor where he sleeps with Niesha. He is by Gabe's mom at her bedside barking. She wakes up startled and says, "Rusty, what's wrong?"

Rusty runs to the stairs going up to Nee's room.

Gabe's mom yells, "What's wrong! Is it something with Nee?"

Even though he's a dog, Emma always felt Rusty could understand her. She hurriedly follows Rusty up the stairs. By this time Nee is awake and meets them at the stairs.

"What's going on?" she asks.

"I don't know, Nee. Rusty came down and woke me up. I thought something was wrong with you. He brought me up the stairs."

"I'm fine," responds Nee. She looks at the golden retriever. "Hey, big guy, what's going on?"

Rusty barks incessantly and runs towards Gabe's old room and stands there barking.

"Rusty, enough of this nonsense! It's the middle of the night!" says Emma.

Rusty won't stop. He actually grabs Nee by the sleeve and pulls her into Gabe's room. She acquiesces and follows. He goes to the window by the fire escape and keeps barking.

Nee hesitates. You could tell she's thinking hard. She trusts Rusty with all her heart. The bond between a human and a dog seems to be telepathic at times, each knowing the other's needs. This was one of those times. She grabs her mom's arm and runs towards the window.

"Go Nee! Go Mom!" yells Gabe.

At this point they're committed. As illogical as it seems, they follow Rusty. There's no physical sign of impending danger, but still, they go on climbing out the window and down the fire escape. They follow Rusty to the back of the yard right by the fence. A subway train goes by just as the house explodes in a huge ball of flame. They're pushed against the fence by the force of the explosion. Miraculously, other than some scrapes and bruises, they're okay. The portal closes down.

I looked at Gabe. "Damn that was close."

He's furious. "That bastard! He almost killed them all. Why can't he leave us alone? I can't do anything to help them!"

"I'm just glad that your dog has a keen sense of smell."

"Yeah, I was thinking about that. How was he able to smell the gas on the third floor before it hit the flame? It seems like a stretch to me."

"I just know that dogs have incredible olfactory ability," I say. "They smell things for which we have no awareness."

"Even so, how did he know to get them out the fire escape? If they went down the stairs, they would be dead now."

"I don't know Gabe, I don't know."

I don't see Gabe for a while. I figure he wants some space, so I back off. As time passes, however, I realize I miss him and am a little worried. I decided to look for him. Again, as it always seems to happen in Afterland, I'm suddenly with him. He's on a basketball court that appears to be in his old neighborhood. He's alone shooting at a metal backboard with a chain link net. It seems to be next to a school as there are also painted lines on the macadam for other sports such as four square, tennis, and volleyball.

I didn't say anything, just start grabbing rebounds and feeding him at the top of the key. He has a nice jumper and a smooth dribble, naturally athletic. I shoot a bit myself and he finally breaks the silence.

"Nice shot for an old white guy."

"Thanks. I may have been six-three, but definitely had White man's disease. I had the vertical leap of a snail."

After a pause I say, "Sorry about your family and your house, man. That sucks."

"Yeah. I just wish I could help them out."

"They really are strong people, Gabe. Losing your dad and then you. Now this shit. I don't think I could hold up."

"None finer than Mom and Nee," says Gabe.

We drop back into a friendly silence and continue to shoot hoops.

Bob pops up. We feel him before we turn towards half court. "What are you doing?" he asks.

"Just shootin' some hoops, Bob. It relaxes me," Gabe says.

"Can I shoot too?"

"Don't see why not. Here you go." Gabe sends a bounce pass Bob's way.

The ball sticks to Bob's bubble and he just holds it there for a minute. Finally, he turns to the hoop and the ball flies over the backboard bouncing off the school wall and back past half court.

"A little strong there, big guy. We might need to work on your touch."

I chase the ball down. We all continue to shoot and soon Bob seems to get more of the hang of things.

"How 'bout some two on two?" I ask Gabe.

"Dude, I know math isn't your strong point, but don't ya think we are missing something?"

"I got an idea." I toss the ball in the air to my right and a blurry version of Michael Jordan caught it at its apex. "I got MJ."

"Bitch, that's not fair," complains Gabe.

"Hey, you get Bob."

"Great!" Then he quickly adds, "Sorry Bob."

I take the ball out and immediately pass off to Jordan. He does a quick juke around Gabe and drives in for a reverse dunk.

"Sweet!" I say as Gabe gave me the finger.

We're up twelve to zero. MJ and I have to switch on defense and Gabe scores on me. Bob pretty much floats around. He passes off to Gabe, but just watches MJ a lot. I started cheating to help out on D against Gabe, not that MJ needs help. Gabe passes the ball to Bob. I drop back to cover him and get housed. Out of nowhere, Bob feigns left and spins around my right side so fast I'm left holding my jock (figuratively of course). He goes to the hoop and jumps impossibly high, hangs for a few seconds and then slams the ball through the rim.

My jaw drops, and Gabe just says, *"Sheeiiiit!"*

I always kinda think of Bob as a cross between a big teddy bear and a bean bag chair. I'm going to have to rethink that one!

From then on, the game changes. Jordan covers Bob and I stick to Gabe. Bob is a fast learner to say the least. He and MJ go toe-to-toe as Gabe and I do our best to stay out of the way. Occasionally, we get a no-look pass thrown our way. Whenever we have the ball, Gabe usually schools me.

Pretty soon we're tied at twenty, and next basket wins. I take the ball out and dribble to my right, throwing a lob pass back to Jordan. Even though he's blurry, he has that look, you know, the '89 playoffs against the Cavs, game five, three seconds to go and down by one. I start to feel bad for Bob; no chance he'll stop MJ.

Jordan pushes into Bob, backing him up a bit. Dribbling with his left, he wraps his right arm backwards around Bob, setting him up for a spin move and fade. Bob gives him a few inches, then follows him right around. Jordan changes direction and moves the ball to his right hand, spinning the opposite direction. No mere mortal could have countered that move, as we had seen so many times in his career. But Bob is no mere mortal. Bob spins right with him as Jordan rises for his classic jumper. Bob somehow gets a piece of the ball and it deflects to Gabe. I'm on him tight, but he easily spins around and throws an alley-oop back to Bob who is floating above the rim. The chain shakes as he jams it home.

"Sweet!" yells Gabe triumphantly.

CHAPTER 16

SOMETIME LATER, I NOTICE a few entities zooming by in a row. I ask Gabe about it.

"Oh, yeah. Someone built a roller coaster up here."

"*W . . . T . . . F?*" I actually say the three letters separately. "Can we ride it?"

"Sure," replies Gabe.

"Hey Gabe, has Bob ever ridden it?"

"No, come to think of it, I don't think he ever has."

"Let's see if he wants to try."

Then of course Bob pops up next to us. With Snoopy.

"Hey Bob, do you want to try the roller coaster?" I ask.

"What's a roller coaster?"

"It's better we show you," says Gabe.

We head over to the start. We just kinda know where it is, and there are no lift stations or lines. I have Bob get in the front with Snoopy, and Gabe and I are right behind him. We start upwards slowly.

I ask Gabe, "Why don't we just go?"

"Well we could, but I like the anticipation. That's always been a favorite part for me. But we could also just start with a magnetic impeller if you wanted."

"No, this is fine for me."

We seem to go up and up forever, but in reality it's probably just a couple minutes. The drop is incredible. We accelerate like Jeff Gordon coming off the fourth turn at Daytona. The hill seems to have no bottom. Finally, we start a slight curve to the right coming up into the next hill. The curve transitions into a double-barrel roll inside a large 360-degree loop. We spiral inside and outside then reverse and enter the loop itself. We hear a noise from Bob that's hard to define, but the closest it resembles is the insurance commercial with Maxwell the Pig going *Weeeeeee!* Snoopy seems to be having a great time also.

I wondered if the ride has an Immelmann loop and sure enough, as soon as I think of it, it happens. The ride goes on and on, the smoothest I ever experienced. Bob's in heaven—pun intended.

Just as we finish zooming along, a portal opens. Unfortunately, not a good one for me. We look down to see my daughter Chloe and my granddaughter Anne in the pediatric ICU. This is a depressive place, but only because of the sick children. The staff and providers are the best medicine has to offer, performing miracles in the face of the unfathomable sorrow. I just don't know how they do it. When I did my rotation in medical school on our pediatric oncology ward, I almost didn't make it. Watching children suffer and die drains you to the core.

The ICU at Columbia has cubicles with machines and monitors everywhere, all of them scaled down like the mini kitchen set that my daughter had when she was growing up. Anne's on a ventilator with four doctors around her. I figure right away that she had a blast crisis with hypoxia and respiratory failure. Though ALL has a good prognosis with a 90 percent survival rate, all leukemia patients can develop acute problems with a sudden rise in their white blood cell count. These are usually immature or *blast* cells that proliferate. The extra cells most often affect the small blood vessels in the lungs and the brain, causing breathing problems or confusion, which can lead to a coma. At this point, I'm sure she had already been on hydroxyurea and chemotherapy.

I hear the providers talking about setting up leukapheresis. While all this is taking place, I see that Anne's not doing well. Chloe separates from the group of doctors and holds her daughter's hands. Just then she flatlines and all hell breaks loose. The nurses and doctors spring into action, working on instinct. I watch as it unfolds but know the outcome. Chloe also seems to sense the inevitable. She backs off into a corner and puts her head in her hands. I can't watch anymore.

The next portal is of Anne's funeral. It's brutal, but I feel I need to be there in order to support Chloe. Child funerals just suck. No other way to say it. Emotions are incredibly high, mostly sorrow, of course, but a lot of anger, confusion, and all the stages of Kubler Ross going on. Her brother is there. He's about age six now and doesn't know really what was going on. The tiny coffin is closed and decorated with pink flowers. I know my daughter is strong, but this is going to be the hardest thing she will ever have to experience. Gabe and Bob are next to me; I sense their presence. We embrace, somehow, even without any arms. Snoopy's at my side also, as he has been so many times when we were growing up. It's comforting to have them all here. Nobody says anything.

CHAPTER 17

EVEN IN AFTERLAND, YOU can get depressed.

I really got in a funk after my granddaughter died and have been moping around, as much as a bubble can mope. Gabe is also a bit down, still trying to get over the near miss his sister and mother just went through.

Suddenly, Gabe and I find ourselves on a vast ocean. Only, it isn't an ocean. The fluid under us is more viscous than water, a dark purple. I notice we're standing on small boards similar to the skim boards that you glide across on the edge of the water at the beach. I get the feeling they are similar to training wheels for bikes. Of course, Bob is with us. Gabe and I are both a bit freaked out. *How can these little boards hold us up?* I also note that there are huge waves building up.

"Uh, Bob. Where are we? What's going on?" I ask.

"This is fun," he says.

Gabe and I beg to differ. We're both stressing. A large wave comes right for us.

Bob isn't fazed at all. He floats right for it. He doesn't need the training boards that we have. We follow despite our trepidation. The wave builds up under us and lifts us to the top. It's impossibly high and now we're both scared shitless.

Bob says, "Come on!" and drops down the swell.

As we look over the incredibly steep hill, I'm reminded of a time when I stood at the top of a double black diamond ski slope with the front half of my skis hanging out over thin air.

Gabe and I exchanged looks of pure horror and simultaneously say, "No fucking way."

Just then, Snoopy pushes us off the side.

I won't repeat the words that came out of our mouths. Surprisingly, we stay upright and follow Bob down the steep slope. Our rate of drop is not as I would expect, and it suddenly hits me that Bob's world has a completely different level of gravity. We quickly get the hang of it and are soon carving up the face. Bob's really ripping it. He pulls an Ollie to catch some air and then spins around backwards with a perfect fakie. As we all get about halfway down the wave, it curls above us into an impossibly large tube. We shoot the barrel, each taking turns in the lead until finally Bob gets in the pocket and leaves us behind like the kooks we are. When we trough out, Bob immediately leads us up to the next peak.

I think, *just what the doctor ordered.*

Such days make me think, *is this really Heaven?* What I know for sure is that life, or should I say *afterlife*, continues in Afterland. This place is so different from all the descriptions we hear as children, but that's not surprising. After all, how does anyone really know what happens when our life ends? Faith can be very strong, however, and I knew a lot of people who had an incredibly strong belief in a heaven.

For some people, passing out of the world is actually a type of relief. Some martyrs seem to actively seek death. At times it can be in noble sacrifice to help others, but also, perversely, can be a crazed suicide bomber who feels that killing others will guarantee an entry to paradise. An act of pure evil that is supposed to bring good to you. No matter what the religion or background, I just can't see the logic of that rationale.

As I ponder these deep questions, Gabe pops up.

"Hey Mike, come over here. Check this out!" He's excited.

I see Bob and Snoopy near a new coaster.

"Hey, wait a minute," I say. "Is that the Cyclone??"

"You bet man, I built it myself."

"Cool! Have you ridden it yet?"

"No, we were waiting for you. Come on, let's get on it."

The real Cyclone has only one line. You can't wait separately in a special que for the front seat. Everyone waits, and seating is just luck of the draw. I kind of liked that. No *Fast Pass*; no special exceptions. If you want to get the front you had to keep riding until you got lucky. Some people would ride the coaster all summer and never get in the front seat. Afterland has its advantages, however, and we're able to get right in the lead car. Gabe and I get in the front seat and Bob and Snoopy are right behind us.

The Cyclone is a full gravity ride. A brake holds the cars in place until passengers are loaded. When the operator releases the lever, the cars descend a shallow ninety-degree turn to get to the lift hill.

The chain grabs us, and we jerk up the hill. Gabe even manages to mimic the sound of the chain as we climb. It isn't a long ride, but it still remains the ultimate classic. As we peak the top at eighty-five feet, we see the boardwalk with its small shops and the expanse of the beach with the Atlantic gleaming from the sun. Off to the right is the pier and the skeleton of the old parachute jump ride. They never took it down when it closed, and it's a Coney Island icon now. After we crest, the coaster continues straight to the first drop of sixty degrees. At the bottom, going about sixty miles an hour, we pass right under another section of the track. Everyone ducks reflexively from the illusion, but we're never really close to hitting our heads. The train rises to a U-turn to the left, and after a quick drop, climbs the second highest hill at seventy feet. This leads to another U-turn at the top, which drops to a camelback with negative G's. Bob likes that! Another U-turn takes us under the first curve, followed by more camelbacks and small hops. Finally, it returns to the station with the brake throwing us into our seatbelts.

As we come back to the station, Bob just says, "Again."

CHAPTER 18

I AM JUST CHILLIN' thinking about an old family vacation, when Gabe appears and says he saw Daemon in a portal.

"What happened?" I ask. "I hope he got struck by lightning."

"He was killed," Gabe says flatly.

"What happened?"

"Street justice. He made some more threats to my family. Some guys who lived in our neighborhood just took him down. They weren't going to wait for the police to do nothing or another joke of a trial after he killed Dee or my mom."

"I'm glad," I say, thinking, *is it wrong to kill evil? Is it wrong to end evil?* Another philosophical question that bugs me.

Thou shall not kill, The fourth of the ten commandments. Does this mean we should never kill? Self-defense can be very subjective. And what about war? What about killing pure evil? By doing so, you might prevent others from being hurt or killed. If "Thou shall not kill" is an absolute, evil would rule the world. Let me give an extreme example.

A man has your child tied to a chopping block with her neck exposed. He has an axe over his head and is starting to swing it down. You are ten feet away with a loaded gun. You can't get to him in time to stop him. Your only hope to prevent the death of your child is to shoot him in the head. Do you pull the trigger? Every parent would say yes. If true evil exists, we need to be able to destroy it.

In the midst of my internal debate a bad portal opens for me.

Chloe walks onto the George Washington Bridge. It's a large suspension bridge across the Hudson River with two levels of two-way traffic and happens to be located just north of her apartment. It's a cold fall night. Even though it is the world's busiest motor vehicle bridge, there isn't much traffic now, so I know it must be either really late or early in the morning before rush hour. There's a bicycle path and pedestrian walkway on the upper deck of the south side of the bridge. On the north they're building eleven-foot-high fences to prevent suicides which, unfortunately, have been fairly common on the bridge.

Chloe is sitting on the outside of the guard rail, looking down at the water more than two hundred feet below. I feel her sadness. I'm sure it has a lot to do with Anne's death, but there are probably other stressors going on to compound things.

I yell, "Gabe, Bob! Help me!" They appear instantly.

"You gotta help me. I think my daughter is going to kill herself!"

"Damn," says Gabe. "What can we do? I could never get through to my family after I died. I tried to console them but never could do anything. I wish we could."

Bob doesn't say anything. He just looks intensely at the portal.

Chloe stands and balances over the edge. The wind is from the south and holds her up. It's strong enough to keep her on the bridge even if she leans forward a little, which she's doing.

"Noooo!" I cry out, burying my head in my hands.

Just then, Chloe's cell phone dings out a text. We all freeze, including Chloe. It's the middle of the night, and the last thing she's expecting is a text. She leans back and looks at her phone curiously. We all see one word on the phone. It says, *DON'T.*

Chloe immediately looks to see who it is. Could her husband have figured out what she was doing? No, that's impossible. He thinks she's at the hospital on call. Also, there's no sender identified on her phone, something that never happens. There's usually a name or at least a phone number.

Gabe and I are also perplexed.

"What the hell?" I say.

We both turned and look at Bob who says nothing. He sems to be more intense, if that makes any sense.

We turn back to the portal and see Chloe back up on the edge again. Whatever she thought of the text, she is so far into the abyss of depression that it isn't going to stop her. It looks like even Bob—if it was Bob that sent that text—can't help her now. She leans forward again.

Suddenly, we hear barking.

WTF!

A small brown dog runs up the side of roadway on the bridge unfazed by the cars whizzing by. He jumps up on the edge of the road barrier and into the startled arms of my daughter. She immediately falls back towards the barrier and starts crying. It's as if years of tears were all coming out at once. She holds the small dog and keeps saying, "Skippy," over and over, rocking him in her arms.

The portal closes, but I know Chloe will be alright.

I look at Gabe. "What just happened?"

"I'm not sure man. I'm guessing that was their dog?"

"Yes, Skippy. But it doesn't make any sense. How did he get out of the courtyard? It's fenced in. Even if he dug out, how did he know where to go? Even if he did all that, he would have had to leave way before Chloe got out of her car and walked onto the bridge to get there when he did. I don't get it."

"I can't help you," says Gabe.

We both look at Bob.

He just says, "Roller coaster."

CHAPTER 19

OCCASIONALLY, I ROAM AROUND our sphere, as I come to think of the *level* that we're in. You have the ability to go up a little but not far. When you try to go outwards, you see fewer entities, and the background scenes lack much definition. Eventually, they stop completely. You have to travel quite a distance, but when you don't see any more entities, you hit a stop. It's not a wall, more like the outside of a bubble. It bends a bit but does not let you through, nor can it be broken—at least not by Gabe or me. When you push on the bubble wall, you can't really see anything in the distance. Sometimes, I think I sense something. I know it's evil, but I can't explain why I know.

Gabe and I ask Bob about it.

"It's the bad place," he says in his usually succinct manor.

"Can people get closer to it?" I ask.

"Why would you want to do that?" asks Bob, truly puzzled.

"I guess it's just our curiosity. It's one of the things that can get us humans into trouble a lot. Occasionally it leads to great and wonderful discoveries, but it can at times lead us to where we shouldn't be."

"This is a place you should not be," Bob says with an inflection that conveys *conversation over!*

Gabe, Bob, Snoopy, and I are now hanging out in an ice cream parlor. I know, pretty screwy. It's an older wooden building in the mountains overlooking a lake. It could be anywhere, but for some reason, it feels like upstate New York. You never really know though.

Half of the building houses the kitchen and self-serving areas. The other half is a large deck open to the sky that is built around two trees protruding right up through the middle. Small tables and chairs are scattered around. We float around one.

"Bob," I ask, "are all of your kind the same?"

"What do you mean?" he answers, always one to clarify.

"Well, are the others from your world all the same color, the same shape, the same size?"

"Why would that matter?" he says, once again getting to a place that humans seem to never be able to reach.

"It doesn't," I say. "In our world we are essentially all built alike inside but have different sizes, features, and colors externally. Unfortunately, it has led to certain people being persecuted, isolated, or even killed because they didn't look like others."

"That's stupid," Bob huffs.

"Yeah, but our world could never get it straight," adds Gabe. "We still have people dying and suffering only because of the color of their skin."

"Was your world ever like that?" I ask Bob.

Bob pauses. Just then, another entity with a similar aura to Bob appears. Bob introduces him as his friend, but his name is incomprehensible in our language. We decide to call him Fred.

Fred immediately starts talking as if he had been a part of the conversation from the beginning.

"I have been here for many times. Way before Bob got here. That is why he summoned me. Our world once had only two types of entities. The difference between the two was very hard to determine. It had to do with the texture of a small protuberance— some of us had small ridges and others had none. Unless you would check very closely, it was impossible to tell us apart. Despite this, our peoples knew the difference and gradually segregated into two groups— the ridgers and the non-ridgers. As Bob has mentioned . . . very stupid. The two groups gradually started to physically separate themselves and each started to feel superior to the other."

"Wait a minute!" I yell. "That's a friggin' Dr. Seuss story!"

"Yeah, you're right man. It's *The Sneetches,*" adds Gabe.

Fred just looks at us blankly.

"A children's author in our world wrote a story exactly like that," I say. "Except the difference was a star on the belly."

I have a thought. "Fred, have you ever met Dr. Seuss?"

"Yes," he says. "Teddy and I have had many nice talks. He is a very wise man."

"Well I'll be damned," I say softly.

"May I continue?" asks Fred. "Anyway, fights broke out and one group was able to gain control of the other. That was the darkest time of our world. A whole group of us was subservient to the others without the rights or equalities that should have been inherent. Bad things happened and a lot of us died. Finally, a small subset of the larger group balked against what had become our normal. They questioned the very core of their beliefs. They basically said—I am going to use a term that Bob learned from you—'This is fuckin' bullshit!'"

"Oops," I say. "That's not really nice language, even though it's appropriate."

"Hey, that's on us man," Gabe says. "But I think it hits the nail on the head." He turns back to Fred. "What happened next?"

"The anger built up on both sides, not just from us. It finally affected change. Respect and trust build up slowly but with traction. The ridgers and non-ridgers interacted more and more, bonding in similar interests and goals. By the time Bob was alive, we were a world of completely different beings. Each of us had evolved depending on our likes and needs. Externally every one of us was different—different sizes, different colors, different shapes. None of that matters anymore. The external shell is superfluous to us."

Gabe and I look at each other. "We have a lot of work to do on our world." I say solemnly.

"Amen," adds Gabe.

CHAPTER 20

THINGS HAVE BEEN BENIGN for a while. No bad portals for Gabe or me. (I always wonder if Bob had portals. I need to ask him that.) No good portals either. I guess things are just cooking along back on Earth. Just as I am teetering on the edge of boredom, a portal opens. It's a good one for both me and Gabe.

Chloe is being honored at Columbia for a research breakthrough. It has to do with CRISPR technology developed to treat leukemia. CRISPR stands for clustered regularly interspaced short palindromic repeats. It's a family of DNA sequences in the genetic makeup of certain organisms. They are derived from bacteriophages—think of these as hunter killer viruses that enter a bacteria and replicate within like a parasite. They use the bacteria's DNA to create replicas of themselves and eventually explode out of the cell to carry on their cycle with other bacteria. It all sounds kind of Machiavellian, but the CRISPR sequences of DNA are actually able to detect and destroy the DNA of the infecting bacteriophages, which in turn protects the bacteria. Used along with certain enzymes, CRISPR sequences can edit the genes within organisms. This is the key to a potentially new way of treating and preventing diseases, including genetic disease like leukemia. A pretty big deal, if you ask me.

I'm surprised when I see Gabe's sister Nee up there right next to Chloe. It turns out, Nee is a medical student working primarily on Chloe's research. Chloe's son and husband are there, of course. Her son seemed to be hanging out with Nee some, but I don't think anything of it.

Gabe and I sit there watching the presentation and the reception. Of course I say we were *sitting*, but as noted, we can't really sit in our current form. Anyway, it's a great day. *Damn it! - NO DAYS in the Afterland!* Anyway, Gabe and I grin a lot.

"I wonder if this was why we connected with each other?" I ask Gabe.

"I don't know man. I think we met way before they started working together."

"Yeah, you're right. It's just weird that our families are connected this way on Earth."

"Small universe, huh?" says Gabe. We both break up laughing.

CHAPTER 21

AS I HAVE MENTIONED before, sometimes up here in Afterland, you just sense things that you have no idea why or how you do. This is one time. Both Gabe and I sense in at the same time. It's a big deal. Everyone around us senses it too.

There's pressure from the outer rings where the evil lurks. We go to the end of the bubble and, for the first time ever, actually see something—not just sense it. There's a mass coalescing in the distance. It's huge and seems to be coming closer, morphing in the distance like an amoeboid thunderhead on the plains of Kansas. Its extremities reach out in all directions, but mostly towards us. We look at each other and say, "WTF?" We do that a lot in Afterland.

As we all budge against the end of the bubble, we sense presences behind us. I see innumerable entities from the inner cores streaming past us. Bob and his species are the vast majority. Then we see Jesus, Mohammed, and Abraham go by. Even Rosa

Parks! Many others, some of whom I recognize and others whom I don't, parade by too. I notice Gandhi and Doswell aren't among them. You gotta respect their pacifism, even if you don't agree with it. Chief Joseph was also missing, holding true to his promise that he would *fight no more forever.*

They rush past us and out the bubble. Gabe and I try to follow them but are stopped. I am not sure by what. We just can't go any farther. After Bob and the others pass, Gabe and I notice that the bubble has expanded. Though we can't get past it, it seemed to stretch much farther. We see everything now, clearly.

"You motherfucker!" Gabe yells as he lurches toward the end of the bubble.

I didn't know what was going on, but I threw myself right along with him, trying to breach the bubble.

"What's the matter? I ask Gabe.

"It's Daemon! . . . You bastard!" he yells, beating his hands on the end of the bubble.

No matter how hard we try, we can't break through to join Bob.

A large three-dimensional battlefield emerges. It doesn't have landmarks or a background. It's only defined by the masses of entities coming together. Just like in a portal, we see things from many perspectives. Bob seems to be the spearhead, along with his friends. They hit the legions of evil directly in their center. We notice other spearheads circling to the left and right, similar to Hannibal's classic move taught in military schools across the world. Hit the center to draw the defenders in and try to outflank them.

Of course, Daemon and his evil hoard know this tactic too. They absorb Bob's frontal attack while sending counter attacks above and below the fanning movements. The fighting is intense. Gabe and I see entities disappearing on both sides. I look at Gabe and wonder, *is this real death? Do those who don't survive now truly go to oblivion?*

The battle rages, with counters to counters on both sides.

As happens in Afterland, the smells of the battle are hyper-intensified—a mix of copper and cordite. We see Bob fighting intensively in the pocket surrounded on every side, top and bottom, by the evil. It looks like the evil is gaining an upper hand as Bob's pocket of resistance shrinks, while the evil seems to be expanding.

Gabe and I push harder at the bubble. We want to help somehow.

Just then, a new two-pronged assault starts by more of Bob's kind. They attack from the very top center and bottom center of the battlefield. From Bob's position, we see a sudden massive release expand out. Gabe and I realize, both suddenly, that this newfound force is all dogs—as in canines—that had been hiding amongst Bob's brethren. They fight with a passion and intensity that only dogs can. Dogs can be intensively loyal and immensely protective, and canine force is surely that. They push out, effectively splitting the evil in two. The dogs give Bob's force a new vigor. As a result, the evil keeps *popping,* with their numbers getting smaller and smaller. We also see a lot of the evils flee to outer regions. Evil can have strength, but it is also filled with cowardice.

As the tide of the battle turns, it now a clear victory for us. We see Bob and Daemon paired off in the center. They collide with a large flash. When the lights dim, Daemon is gone. But so is Bob! Gabe and I are devastated. Bob is family.

The fighting is winding down. The evil beings are either retreating or disappearing rapidly. Finally, they're gone. It's a full victory, but a costly one.

We watch as our brethren all came back through the bubble. Their numbers are greatly diminished. The mood is somber.

"Do you see Bob?" I ask Gabe.

"No."

"Damn."

The dogs, Bob's kindred, and those in the inner circle, keep passing by. We see Fred. He's weak but recognizes us.

"Where's Bob? Is he all right?" we ask.

Fred slows and looks at us. "I don't know," is all he says and turns to head back with the others.

We continue watching, a sick feeling building within us. We scrutinize every entity that passes by, looking for any sign of Bob. Finally, the parade of warriors trickles to a stop and vanishes. We're now alone at the barrier but still can't tear ourselves away. After what felt like forever, I start to turn slowly back towards the inner sphere.

Just then Gabe cries out, "Look!"

We both know it's Bob, even though his aura and size seem diminished. We reach to pull him through the bubble. He's weak but recognizes us immediately. We pull him close. I can tell he's struggling, and seems to be getting weaker.

"Bob, what can we do? How can we help? . . . Tell us, man!" says Gabe.

Bob, true to himself, says little.

"Roller coaster," he whispers.

I create a hanging coaster based on the Gatekeeper at Cedar Point Amusement Park in Sandusky, Ohio. The park was built on a long spit of land that extended out into Lake Erie. Originally, it was only accessible by ferry boats but has since been connected by a causeway. The park takes up most of the end of the peninsula and is surrounded by the lake. The Gatekeeper is located on the northern coast against the beach and just east of the large Breakers Hotel originally built in 1905. It is one of the smoothest coasters you could ever experience. The seats hang to the sides of the track making you feel like you are truly flying as you experience the loops and gentle curves.

Bob is so small now that he fits in a seat right between us. Oddly, Snoopy is nowhere around. He never leaves Bob's side. When I asked about him, Bob just turns away.

The lift is smooth, the first hill gentle with an arch to the right. We ride into a spiral loop then a long gentle drop to the left. At the bottom we do a long vertical loop that seems like it never ends. I notice that the scenery changes. The views of Lake Erie and the rest of the park morph into a world I could never have imagined. The sky is a red-to-pink hue with no clouds. As we take another gentle-sweeping turn left, we notice some kind of vegetation unlike anything we had ever seen, colored purple and orange with some yellow. The *trees* if you could call them that, are impossibly tall and interact with each other in a symbiotic way. I notice that what looks like rocks are actually alive. They move in a fluid fashion, subtlety yet constantly changing shapes. Just then, we hit a loop with a half twist to the right. We encounter a waterfall that's the same stuff we had surfed on. It cascades off the top shooting out about fifty feet before starting a gentle arch to the lake at the bottom. Instead of mist there are small droplets like mercury that float skyward. Gabe and I watch in awe. Among the droplets, creatures gracefully twist and glide. These are the ones I had seen before, long and flat, undulating like ribbons. Finally, we do a last spiraling turn and return to the start. As we slow, we both realized that Bob is gone.

CHAPTER 22

GABE AND I MOURN Bob and Snoopy for a long, long time. As is inevitable, afterlife goes on. We eventually create new coasters and occasionally encounter new watch-portals. The evil is still here, but we sense that it is weak and far away. We realize that it would not be a concern to us anytime in the foreseeable future. The problem is that the future was unforeseeable.

A large portal opens. Gabe and I stare in amazement. It's a wedding. It only takes us a minute to realize it's Nee and Billie getting married. Chloe is there, of course, and she's pregnant. I guess the CRISPR therapy works.

Gabe's mom, Emma, and Judi look great, sitting in the front row not aging in the least. Gabe and I sit back and dream up a couple of beers.

The ceremony is perfect. The reception goes on and on. Gabe and I are mentioned in the toasts, and the tears are all happy ones.

"It would have been great if Gabe and Dad knew each other,"

Chloe toasts. "I bet they would have liked each other. I feel like they're with us, watching."

Gabe and I smile. "Indeed," I say.

Just then, appearing in front of me and within reach is a small child, and I immediately sense it is my grandchild. I stare and reach for Anne. I feel my aura brighten, and for a moment it feels like I am holding her.

"She's here to see her family, just like you, Mike," says Gabe. I sense his profound joy and amazement.

The three of us watch, smiling, as the reception winds down. Nee checks her iPhone and gasps. She runs to Billie and shows him. He goes white, as much as a White person can turn white.

Chloe then looks at her phone and gasps, darting over to show Judi. They all just stare.

They walk together to the table where Emma is sitting. They show her the phones. She looks at them intently and then looks towards the ceiling. It seems like she's looking right into our eyes. She smiles.

Gabe and I can then finally see what's on their phones— a picture of Gabe, and me holding Anne.

"Who could have done this?" I ask Gabe. "Bob's gone. Fred's nowhere to be seen."

Suddenly we both instinctively look up and see an aura brighter and more powerful than any I've encountered in Afterland.

"Big Mamma," says Gabe, reverently.

Within Big Mamma's glow is Bob.